CLAIMING MISTER KEMP

EMILY LARKIN

www.emilylarkin.com

Claiming Mister Kemp / Emily Larkin. -- 1st ed.

ISBN 978-0-9941384-7-7

Cover Design: The Killion Group, Inc

❀ Created with Vellum

A Baleful Godmother

Novel

Dear Reader

Claiming Mister Kemp is a romance between two men.

It's a departure from what I usually write, but when Tom and Lucas walked onto the page in *Trusting Miss Trentham,* I liked them both so much that I wanted to discover their story.

This novel does contain several scenes where men engage in sexual intimacies with each other. If such scenes are *not* within your comfort zone, please stop reading here! I have other books you'll enjoy that feature heroines and their heroes. A full list can be found at www.emilylarkin.com/books.

Happy reading,

Emily Larkin

Chapter One

October 6th, 1808
London

LIEUTENANT THOMAS MATLOCK trod briskly up the steps of Albany Chambers and rapped on the door to Lucas Kemp's rooms. The moon shone cold and bright overhead and an icy breeze fingered its way between the folds of his military greatcoat.

His knock sounded loudly—and was followed by silence.

Tom knocked a second time, less hopefully, and then dug in his pocket for the key. He unlocked the door and let himself in to the entrance hall. "Lucas?"

The set of rooms was dark and silent.

He called out again, this time for Lucas's manservant, "Smollet?" and was met with more silence.

Tom sighed, and hefted the bottle in his hand, and debated what to do. Did he want to traipse all over London looking for Lucas? He wasn't dressed for the clubs; he still wore the clothes he'd traveled in all day. *You should have stopped to shave and change, idiot.*

Tom sighed again. He placed the bottle on the little table in the entrance hall, where Lucas could hardly fail to see it when he came in—then picked it up again and ventured into the sitting room, carefully picking his way past dimly seen furniture to the cold fireplace. There, he placed the bottle in the center of the mantelpiece, label facing outwards. "Happy birthday, Lu," he said quietly.

Someone muttered behind him.

Tom jerked around.

The sitting room was dark, and beyond it was the entrance hall, and beyond that, the open door and the courtyard. The distant lamplight made the rooms as black as the inside of a tomb.

As black—but not as silent. His ears caught the sound of someone breathing.

The hair on Tom's scalp pricked upright. "Hello?" he said cautiously, and then—because this *was* Lucas's sitting room and who else but Lucas would be here?—"Lucas? Is that you?"

The muttering came again, like a man talking in his sleep.

Tom strode out to the entrance hall, found the chamberstick and tinderbox where Smollet always left them, lit the candle and returned to the sitting room. The shadows retreated to the corners, showing him the familiar furniture: tables and chairs, desk and bookcases. Lots of bookcases, because Lucas liked reading even more than he liked boxing and riding.

Two winged armchairs had long ago staked out territory on either side of the fireplace, hulking leather beasts with brass studs burnished from years of use. In the nearest one, a man slouched, eyes shut, chin sunk on his chest.

"Lucas? What the devil are you doing here in the dark?"

But he could answer that question himself: Lucas was drunk. A *lot* drunk.

"Where's that man of yours?" Tom demanded. "Smollet?"

Lucas's eyelids rose heavily. He stared at Tom without recognition, blinked twice, and closed his eyes.

"Hello, Tom," Tom said, under his breath. "Welcome back to England, Tom. Nice to see you again, Tom." He bent and spoke close to Lucas's ear: "Where's Smollet, Lu?"

Lucas was usually punctilious about his appearance. No one would ever call him a peacock—he liked sober colors and plain tailoring—but he was always immaculate, almost fastidiously so. Not tonight. His guinea-gold hair stuck up in tufts, his collar-points had wilted, and he wore no neckcloth at all. Fumes wafted from him. Cognac, judging from the smell. Tom peered at Lucas more closely in the candlelight. Moisture glinted on his cheeks, glinted in his eyelashes. Lucas wasn't just drunk; he'd been crying.

Tom had seen soldiers cry after battle. Hell, he'd cried himself, a couple of times. But a man's tears had never had quite this effect on him before. His throat tightened and his heart seemed to clench inside his ribcage.

He cleared his throat and shook Lucas's shoulder roughly. "Where's that damned man of yours?"

Lucas's eyelids flickered again.

"Smollet, Lu. Where is he?" *And what the devil does he mean by leaving you here in the cold and the dark?*

"Gave 'im the night off," Lucas muttered.

Tom straightened, and sighed. "Then I guess it's up to me to put you to bed."

TOM CLOSED THE door to the courtyard, lit two more candles,

and went into Lucas's bedchamber, where he kindled the fire, turned back the covers, and set one candle on the bedside table. Then he returned to the sitting room and stared down at Lucas, sprawled in the armchair, disheveled and drunk. It didn't take any feat of insight to guess why Lucas had chosen to spend his twenty-seventh birthday like this. The solitude, the alcohol, the tears were because of his dead twin sister, Julia.

Tom shook Lucas's shoulder gently. "Come on, Lu. Time for bed."

Lucas hunched away from his hand. "Go 'way," he mumbled, not opening his eyes.

Tom uttered a faint laugh. This wasn't the welcome he'd imagined. "No. I'm staying until you get into bed."

"Want t' be alone."

"Tough. I'm not Smollet. You can't tell me what to do." He took Lucas's arm and tried to haul him from the armchair.

Lucas pulled free. His eyes slitted open. He clumsily swung a blow.

"Easy, man," Tom said, catching the fist.

Lucas's eyes came fully open, his fist clenched in Tom's hand—and then Lucas blinked, and bafflement crossed his face. His fist sagged. He peered at Tom owlishly. "Tom? That you, Tom?"

"Yes. Come on, on your feet."

Lucas's brow creased with confusion. "You're in Portugal."

"No, you cod's head, I'm right here. On your feet." He hauled on Lucas's arm again, and this time Lucas didn't try to strike him.

Lucas was six foot two and built like a prizefighter, but Tom was two inches taller, and if he was leaner than Lucas, he was almost as strong. A grunt and a mighty heave and he had Lucas on his feet.

"You're in Portugal," Lucas said again, swaying.

"I'm back for the inquiry into the Convention of Cintra."

"Huh?"

"I'll explain it later." *When you're not drunker than a sailor*. He slung Lucas's slack arm over his shoulder. "Come on. Bed."

Lucas couldn't walk a straight line. Not only that, his legs kept buckling. Tom was out of breath by the time they reached the bedroom door. "Jesus, Lu, how much cognac did you have?"

"Dunno," Lucas said, and uttered a discreet burp.

"You'd better not shoot the cat," Tom said, warningly.

"Not tha' drunk," Lucas said, leaning bonelessly against him.

"Yes, you are—and I swear to God, Lu, if you vomit on me I'm going to shove you headfirst into the nearest privy."

Lucas huffed a faint, cognac-scented laugh, and then sighed heavily. "I missed you."

Tom tightened his grip on him. *I missed you, too*. He permitted himself to rest his cheek against Lucas's hair for a brief second, and then thought, *Fuck it*, and pressed his face into Lucas's hair and inhaled deeply.

Lucas didn't notice; he was too drunk.

Tom closed his eyes and inhaled two more breaths. Nineteen years of friendship, and this was the closest they'd ever physically been. Almost hugging.

Tom thought about the battlefield, and he thought about musket balls and death, and he thought about all the years he'd loved Lucas and been too afraid to do anything about it. He thought about opportunities missed and opportunities lost, and then he thought, *This time I'm not going to be a coward*. Because this time could be the last time. In fact, this time shouldn't be happening at all. He should be buried in Portugal —but by the damnedest miracle he was still alive, and he was *not* going to waste this chance.

Chapter Two

LUCAS KNEW HE WAS DRUNK, he knew Tom was inexplicably in his rooms, but his thoughts had narrowed to a funnel and there was no space in his head for anything other than not falling over. The bedchamber slowly revolved around him and the bed seemed a very long way away and when he finally reached it, it took all his effort to sit upright on the edge and not collapse in a heap.

"Boots," Tom said, and Lucas clutched the bedcovers and managed not to fall over when Tom yanked his boots off. The bed moved up and down like a dinghy and the bedchamber rotated slowly.

After the boots, Tom peeled him out of his coat and waistcoat and hauled the shirt over his head. "Smollet . . . does a . . . better job," Lucas said.

Tom grunted a laugh. "I'm sure he does. Lie down."

Lucas collapsed gratefully on the bed. The mattress rose and fell beneath him and the ceiling spun overhead. He squeezed his eyes shut. *I am not going to throw up.*

7

Lucas drifted away, and while he drifted his thoughts wandered inexorably back to Julia. Julia, with her sharp eyes and exuberant laugh and the way she'd had of knowing exactly what he was thinking.

Grief welled up in him, and with it was the ever-present ache of loss and the sense that part of him had been amputated, that he was missing an arm or a leg.

Dimly, he heard Smollet moving in the bedroom. Lucas closed his ears to the sounds. All he wanted was to be alone.

"All right, let's get these breeches off," someone said. The voice was not Smollet's.

Lucas blearily opened his eyes. The person standing beside the bed wasn't his manservant. This man had a bony, aristocratic face with patrician cheekbones and a high-bridged nose. You could tell just by looking at him that he was a nobleman's son.

Lucas stared at him in fuzzy astonishment. "Tom?"

"That's me," Tom said cheerfully.

"But . . . you're in Portugal."

"Not right now, I'm not."

"What you doin' here?"

"We've already had this conversation, Lu."

Lucas blinked slowly. "We have?"

"You are *so* drunk," Tom said, and he laughed and shook his head. "Come on, Lu. Breeches."

But Lucas's fingers were like bunches of sausages, thick and clumsy. Undoing his buttons was beyond him.

"Let me," Tom said, pushing his hands aside.

Lucas desisted in his efforts. He lay on the bed, his thoughts turning as slowly as the ceiling. Tom was back in England? Tom was unbuttoning his breeches?

Tom was unbuttoning his breeches.

Sudden heat flooded Lucas's groin.

Tom stripped the breeches off, and then the stockings. Lucas groggily realized that he was naked but for his drawers, and that underneath his drawers, his cock was stiffening.

"Drawers, too," Tom said.

Panic stirred in Lucas's chest. *No.* But by the time he'd found his tongue, Tom had unbuttoned the drawers and tugged them down. "No," Lucas said, but Tom had already tossed the drawers on the floor and turned away.

Lucas heaved himself up on one elbow and glanced down at himself. His cock was half erect, the crown peeping rosily from its sheath. His panic grew. Tom mustn't see this. Tom must never guess.

He groped frantically for the bedclothes—a blanket, a sheet, anything—but the bed was tilting under him, and the covers seemed nailed to the mattress, and his cock was growing harder, lunging upright with all the energy of a young bullock.

"Where's your nightshirt? I know I saw it somewhere. Ah, here it is."

Panic strangled the breath in Lucas's throat. He tugged frantically at the bedcovers. *He mustn't see.*

Tom turned around, nightshirt in hand. His gaze flicked to Lucas's groin, and then up to his face.

They stared at each other for an unbreathing moment, a moment that went on so long that Lucas thought he was going to asphyxiate—and then Tom gave a lopsided grin. "Like that, is it?"

"Drunk," Lucas managed to say, horrified. "Happens when I'm drunk." He covered his groin with a hand, shielding himself from Tom's gaze.

"Does it?" Tom stepped closer to the bed, tall and black-haired and still grinning that lopsided grin, the grin that always took Lucas's breath away.

"Nightshirt," Lucas said urgently.

"I think we'd better deal with this first, don't you?" Tom dropped the nightshirt on the floor. "Dashed uncomfortable for you otherwise." He stepped even closer to the bed. His grin faded. His eyes, green and intent, were fixed on Lucas's.

"Nightshirt," Lucas croaked, in desperation.

"Not yet," Tom said, and he pushed Lucas's hand aside and wrapped his fingers around Lucas's cock.

Lucas's whole body jolted. His voice choked in his throat. "Aah . . ."

"Happy birthday, Lu," Tom said, and he bent and took Lucas's cock in his mouth and sucked strongly.

Pleasure surged through Lucas like a river bursting its banks. His bones turned to liquid. He collapsed back on the bed, dizzy with shock, befuddled with alcohol and astonishment. Tom was holding his cock? Tom was sucking him?

Lucas lay helpless, drunk on cognac, drunk on pleasure. The mattress rose and fell beneath him, and the ceiling spun above him, and his heart beat fast and hard in his chest, and each beat was a word, and that word was *Tom*.

Tom touching him. Tom sucking him.

The pleasure and the dizziness built. The mattress swayed like a boat tossed in a storm. The ceiling spun faster. Lucas squeezed his eyes shut against vertigo. His brain felt seasick— but the rest of him was rushing towards climax. His hips were jerking upwards and his hands were clenched in the bedcovers and inarticulate grunts were coming from his throat.

The sound of Tom's name in his ears grew deafeningly loud—*Tom, Tom, Tom*—and then Lucas fell headlong into the most intense orgasm of his life, like a ship plummeting off the edge of the world.

On the heels of that explosion of pleasure came unconsciousness.

Chapter Three

October 7ᵗʰ, 1808
London

TOM CLIMBED THE steps to Lucas's rooms. It was darker than it had been last night, the moon obscured by clouds.

This time, when he knocked on the door, it opened.

"Master Tom?" The manservant's expression transformed to one of delight. "You're back!"

"Hello, Smollet. Lucas in?"

"He's dining with Mr. Howick tonight, sir. He'll be so sorry to have missed you. Are you in town long?"

"A few weeks," Tom said, and then hesitated. "I came round last night. Didn't Lucas tell you?"

"No. Oh— The port wine on the mantelpiece!"

"Best Portuguese."

"I wondered where it had come from. No, sir, he didn't mention your visit."

"He was rather castaway."

Smollet grimaced fleetingly.

Tom looked at the man—stocky and blunt-faced, in his early forties. He'd been with Lucas since Lucas had left the nursery. "May I have a word with you?"

"With me?" Smollet's eyebrows lifted fractionally. "Of course, sir. Come in."

Tom stepped inside. He removed his hat and gloves, gave Smollet his greatcoat, and walked through into the sitting room. Candles glowed in the sconces and a fire burned briskly in the grate.

He glanced at the bedroom door. It was closed.

Tom sat in the armchair Lucas had slouched in last night. A book sat on the table alongside, a ribbon neatly marking Lucas's place.

Smollet came to stand before him. "Sir?"

Tom nodded at the second armchair. "Have a seat, man."

Smollet obeyed. "Sir?" he asked again.

"Tell me how Lucas is."

"He's very well, sir."

"No." Tom waved this answer aside. "How is he? Truthfully."

Smollet hesitated, and then said, "Better than he was."

Tom eyed the man. Smollet was the perfect gentleman's gentleman. Efficient, discreet, sober—and loyal. That was the rub: Smollet's loyalty. He wouldn't gossip about the man he'd dressed since childhood. "Lucas was so drunk last night he couldn't stand up." He wrestled with his own loyalty, and then said, "He'd been crying."

Smollet gave another fleeting grimace, and looked away.

"For God's sake, man. This isn't tattlemongering! I need to know how he is so I can *help* him."

Smollet glanced back at him.

"You said he's better now than he was, so tell me: how *was* he?"

Smollet pressed his lips together, as if holding words back, and then sighed. "He's been pretty bad, Master Tom."

"How bad?"

Smollet looked down at his hands. He smoothed one cuff, then the other. "He's never been a gabster. Not like Miss Julia."

Tom waited.

Smollet sighed again and looked up, meeting his eyes. "He stopped talking after she died. He'd answer if you spoke to him, but otherwise . . . He'd go days without saying a word."

"I saw him in June," Tom said, disturbed. A few hours only, snatched before embarking for Portugal. "He was talking then."

"In public, yes," Smollet said, and lapsed into silence again. But it wasn't the silence of a man who'd said all he wanted to say. The manservant's lips were compressed, his brow faintly knotted, his hands gripped together in his lap.

Wrestling with his loyalty, Tom diagnosed. "Lucas stopped talking," he prompted. "What else?"

Smollet's lips pressed more tightly together, and then he said, "Laudanum."

"Laudanum?"

"We was down in Cornwall—that estate he inherited last year . . ."

Tom nodded encouragingly. "I know of it. Pendarve."

"He wasn't sleeping more'n an hour or two a night, and he was getting worn to the bone, and he started taking laudanum and I thought it was a good thing—because at least it helped him sleep!—but then he started taking more, and he got so he was like a sleepwalker and . . . I didn't know what to do."

Tom listened with alarm. "Is he taking that much

laudanum now?" Had Lucas's confusion last night been due to more than just cognac?

"No, sir." Smollet hesitated, and then said, "I threw it all out."

Tom lifted his eyebrows. "Threw it out?"

Smollet nodded. "Master Lucas was . . . not pleased."

Tom sat back in the armchair and eyed Smollet with respect. "I imagine he wasn't."

"He turned me off."

Tom blinked. Lucas was as devoted to Smollet as Smollet was to him. "He what?"

"I told him as how Miss Julia didn't hold with laudanum, and how she'd be regular worried if she were alive and could see what he was at, and he threw a boot at me and damned me to perdition and turned me off. But an hour later he begged my pardon, and told me I had the right of it, and that he'd be obliged if I would stay after all. You know how he is, Master Tom. He don't stay angry for long, and he always begs one's pardon."

Tom did know. "When was this?"

"Last winter."

"And there's been no more laudanum since then?"

"No more laudanum, but . . . he started dipping pretty heavily."

Tom remembered Lucas last night: too drunk to stand, let alone walk.

"It came about over several weeks. I wasn't worried at first, but then it grew so much that I *was* worried, but there weren't a thing I could say to stop him. Miss Julia didn't have nothing against a drop of wine."

"His family—"

"We was at Pendarve, sir. Weren't no one to notice if he

got castaway every night—and no one but me to care about it."

"Every night?" Tom said, perturbed. Lucas had never been a heavy drinker.

"Used to be. But I packed him into a post-chaise one night when he were too drunk to notice, and took him back to Whiteoaks."

Tom was surprised into a crack of laughter. "How did he take that?"

Smollet smiled ruefully. "I think he would have turned me off again if he hadn't been feeling so poorly."

Tom shook his head, chuckling, and then sobered. "Did it work? Going home?"

"Yes, sir. We stayed for all of April and May, and he didn't get castaway once, and he hasn't since . . . excepting last night, which isn't to be wondered at, seeing as how it were their birthday."

"No," Tom said. "Not to be wondered at."

They were both silent. Tom wondered if Smollet was thinking of Julia, too, thinking of how close she and Lucas had been.

A coal shifted in the grate. Tom gave himself a mental shake. "So that's how he's been . . . how is he *now*?"

Smollet frowned, and pursed his lips, as if deliberating what to say.

"Don't dress it up in clean linen."

Smollet met his eyes and said bluntly, "He put off his blacks and he started talking more, and he *looks* like he's over it, but you know him as well as I do, Master Tom, and you'll see for yourself pretty quick that it's all a sham."

"How much of a sham?"

"He still has days where he don't speak at all. And days where he don't want to leave his bedchamber."

Tom's throat tightened. He looked away, at the fire.

"Miss Julia's been dead more'n a year, but I think he still misses her every minute of every day, and even if he don't take the laudanum anymore or drink himself under the table every night, I think he wants to."

Tom glanced back at the manservant.

"But he won't talk about it, so I'm only guessing." Smollet gave a helpless shrug.

Smollet was no fool; his guess would be a good one.

Tom blew out a breath. "I didn't realize it was so bad."

Smollet didn't respond to this statement of the obvious; instead he said, "How long are you here for?"

"I don't know. No one knows when the inquiry will start, let alone how long it'll go on for." Tom scrubbed a hand through his hair. "I'll see if I can get some leave."

He saw relief on Smollet's face. "That would be good, Master Tom. If you could. He misses you, though he'd never say it."

He did say it yesterday. Tom remembered Lucas sagging against him in the bedroom doorway, a warm, heavy weight. He remembered Lucas's huff of laughter, his sigh, his words: *I've missed you*.

And he remembered Lucas naked and aroused on the bed.

Tom cleared his throat. "He didn't mention my visit last night?"

"No, sir. I doubt he remembers. He had a devil of a head this morning."

Was it a good thing Lucas didn't remember what had happened? Or not?

Chapter Four

Tom found Lucas at Ned Howick's lodgings in Duke Street, with two other friends from their schooldays. The men sat around a table, with a punch bowl and a pack of cards, but when Ned's manservant ushered Tom into the room there was a scraping of chair legs as everyone stood hastily.

"Tom!"

"Matlock, old chap!"

He was clapped on the back, his hand wrung heartily, a chair drawn up to the table for him, a glass of punch poured, the cards shoved aside. Questions were pelted at him about the recent skirmishes in Portugal, the French defeat—and unavoidably, the Convention of Cintra.

"It's a disgrace!" Rupert Banning said indignantly. "Those damned generals should be discharged from the army!"

"Burrard and Dalrymple certainly, but not Wellesley," Tom sipped the punch. It was warm and spicy, potent with arrack. "Wellesley wanted to fight. He was as mad as anything to go after the French."

Talk turned to the approaching hunting season. Tom drank a second glass of punch, refused a third, and kept an eye on Lucas. He looked to be in good spirits, leaning back in his chair, glass in hand.

A sham, Smollet had said. But it didn't look like a sham; it looked real. It looked as if last night—the cognac, the tears in the dark—hadn't happened.

Lucas caught his glance and smiled cheerfully.

He doesn't remember that I found him crying, Tom thought. *He doesn't remember that I put him to bed.*

He dug in his pocket and pulled out his latest sketchbook and a stub of a pencil.

"You still doing that?" Ned asked, as Tom flicked through to the next blank page.

"Whenever I can. Don't mind me. Keep talking."

The four men, inured by long experience to his sketchbook and pencil, did just that. Tom drew them quickly, two-minute portraits, each on a page two and a half inches by four. Rupert Banning, with his collar-points as high as a dandy. John Ludlow, halfway to being drunk. Ned Howick, round-faced and jolly. And Lucas, lounging in his chair.

Tom's pencil slowed. Lucas was nowhere near as relaxed as he appeared. His smile didn't reach his eyes. He looked like a man enjoying a convivial evening with friends, but he wasn't. *Smollet was correct: it's a sham.*

Tom soberly sketched in the folds of Lucas's neckcloth, closed the little book, and tucked the pencil back into his pocket.

"Let's see," Rupert said, with a snap of his fingers.

The sketchbook was passed around the table, and inevitably the pages were turned back to the beginning and the drawings of the past two weeks examined—the journey from

Plymouth, the transport from Lisbon. "This Portugal?" Ned asked, peering at a street scene.

"Lisbon."

"You got any more sketchbooks of Portugal?"

"A couple." He glanced at Lucas. "I brought them to show Lu."

"What? You've got them here?" Ned said. "Show us!"

Tom pushed to his feet and went out into the entrance hall and fished in the pockets of his greatcoat. One, two, three little sketchbooks. He hesitated a moment, and then drew out the fourth, uncertain whether he wanted to show it to anyone.

He brought the books back to the table, laid three of them out, and tucked the fourth one in his pocket, still undecided. "Not much in one of 'em. Spilled tea over it."

Lucas refilled everyone's glasses but his own and the sketchbooks were passed around. The inevitable questions followed: questions about soldiering, about what it was like to be one of General Wellesley's aides-de-camp.

"Where's this?" Ned wanted to know, and "What the devil's this?" John asked, and Tom leaned over the table to explain.

"Who's this?" Lucas asked.

"Let me see." Tom reached across for the sketchbook. "That's Houghton. Damned good sergeant. Lost an arm at Vimeiro, poor sod." He handed the book back. His fingers brushed Lucas's briefly.

Tom reached for his glass and sipped, and watched Lucas study the sketch of Sergeant Houghton.

Lucas was very carefully not looking at him, all his attention on the sketchbook, but Tom wasn't fooled. The angle of Lucas's head, the set of his shoulders . . . it looked like casual nonchalance, but it wasn't. Tom's fingers burned where they'd touched Lucas's, and he knew—*knew*—that Lucas's fingers were burning, too.

Lucas turned three more pages, his gaze fixed on the little book, and Tom made a discovery: Lucas was blushing ever so faintly, the merest hint of color along his cheekbones, almost invisible in the lamplight.

Tom swallowed another mouthful of punch. *He's as aware of me as I am of him.* And on the heels of that thought, came a jump of intuition: Lucas *did* remember what had happened in his bedchamber last night.

He watched Lucas flip through the pages, and told himself that intuition wasn't infallible, that maybe he was seeing what he wanted to see, that the blush was because the room was overly warm, that in all likelihood Lucas didn't remember last night.

"No battle sketches?" Rupert said, flicking through a sketchbook, his tone disappointed.

"There's no time to draw during battle. And if I tried to, the general would have my head on a platter—and rightly so!"

"You'd be a target, standing still," John put in.

"You're a target whether you're standing still or not," Tom said, and he brought out the fourth sketchbook and tossed it down on the table.

"Jesus Christ!" Ned said, reaching for it.

Rupert beat him to it, picking up the book, giving a low whistle. "Musket ball?"

"At Roliça."

"Where were you carrying it?" Rupert asked, turning the sketchbook over in his hand, fingering the lump of lead embedded in it.

"Breast pocket." Tom tapped above his heart. "Knocked me off my horse. I thought I was dead for a few seconds."

John took the sketchbook and examined it. "Lord," he said, awe in his voice. "That's something, that is!"

Tom shrugged, and glanced at Lucas.

Lucas's smile had congealed. If Tom didn't know Lucas had been nursing the same glass of punch for the last hour, he'd think him drunk and ready to cast up his accounts.

TOM STAYED ANOTHER HALF HOUR, and Lucas didn't say a single word, not even when Ned asked him if he'd like more punch. He simply shook his head. Ned and Rupert and John, well on the way to being bosky, didn't notice his silence, but Tom did.

Soberly, he stacked the sketchbooks in a little pile, the one with the musket ball at the bottom. *I shouldn't have let Lucas see it.*

At eleven, Tom pushed to his feet. "I must be off."

"Me, too," John said, yawning and lurching to his feet. "Promised to drop in on Frasier. Coming, Rupert? Lucas?"

Rupert declined.

Lucas stood. "I think I'll head home." He thanked Ned for his hospitality, and donned his coat and gloves. A smile sat on his face, but his eyes gave him away, blue and somber.

Tom silently pulled on his own greatcoat, and wished he'd kept the fourth sketchbook in his pocket.

Outside, thick clouds still covered the moon. John walked as far as Oxford Street with them, then took his leave with a cheerful good-bye, lounging off into the dark. Tom matched his step to Lucas's. "You all right?" he asked quietly.

"Me? Of course."

Bollocks. "Lu . . ." He caught Lucas's arm, halting him. "We need to talk."

Lucas tried to tug free.

21

Tom tightened his grip. "We need to talk."

"Tom, I'm tired. I'm drunk. I just want to go to bed."

"You're not drunk." *You're upset*. He paused, and then said, "Last night you *were* drunk."

Lucas wrenched his arm free. He began striding towards Grosvenor Square.

Tom stretched his legs to catch up. "Last night—"

"I don't remember last night!" Lucas said fiercely.

The devil you don't.

They walked to Grosvenor Square in silence, their boots slapping briskly on the pavement. Tom didn't notice the great townhouses towering against the black sky. He was remembering what it had been like to hold Lucas's cock in his mouth.

Intuition told him that Lucas was remembering it, too. Tension built between them as they walked, a taut, prickling awareness of each other. They turned into Brook Street. Lucas lengthened his stride, walking even faster. Trying to outrun the memory of last night? Trying to outrun the silent, sexual *frisson* between them?

Or is it only me who feels it?

Tom didn't think so. Something—instinct, hunch, gut feeling—call it whatever one wanted—*something* told him that the attraction wasn't one-sided. That it had never been one-sided.

But if Lucas felt the *frisson*, he clearly didn't want to talk about it. He wanted to pretend it didn't exist, to pretend that last night hadn't happened.

I should let this go. It could ruin our friendship.

And then Tom thought of the musket ball, and how close he'd come to death, and thought *Fuck it, I'm not letting this go.*

Lucas swung right and cut down Avery Row, striding fast.

"Lucas—"

"Not now."

"Yes, now." Another five minutes and they'd be at the Albany, where Smollet was waiting and where any chance of private conversation would be lost.

"I told you: I don't—"

The Brook Street Mews loomed to one side, a black cave in the darkness. Tom caught Lucas's arm and pulled him into the mews.

Lucas tried to jerk his arm free. "Look, I don't want to talk. I'm tired—"

"Tough," Tom said, propelling Lucas backwards until his back thudded up against a wall. "Because I *do* want to talk."

"Damn it, Tom—"

Tom leaned in and kissed him. He couldn't see Lucas in the darkness of the mews; the kiss fell off-center, catching the very corner of Lucas's mouth.

Lucas stiffened, and jerked his head back. Tom heard their breaths—short, sharp—and then he kissed Lucas again.

This time he found his mark: Lucas's mouth. Lucas's lips.

Lucas jerked his head back again and made a wordless sound of protest—and Tom's certainty twisted into sick realization that he'd made a mistake, that the attraction *was* one-sided—and then Lucas uttered a sobbing sound and kissed him back.

The kiss was a clash of mouths—rough, fierce, clumsy, desperate. He felt Lucas's fingers dig into his arms, felt their bodies strain against each other.

Tom kissed Lucas until he was breathless and dizzy, until his hat tumbled off, then he gulped a breath and kissed him again—and again—again—years of pent-up desire compressed into a handful of seconds. Each kiss was frantic, savage, hungry, their mouths colliding bruisingly.

Finally he tore free and rested his cheek against Lucas's, gulping air, dizzy with euphoric disbelief. Lucas was panting, too, and shaking. Tom was aware of his own arousal beating in his blood, and he was aware of Lucas's arousal, too. How could he *not* be aware of that pressure against his hip? Lucas's cock, as hard as it had been last night.

Tom fumbled at Lucas's waist, slipping one hand inside his pantaloons.

Lucas made a grab for his wrist. "No."

Tom gave a breathless laugh. "Why not?" He twisted his wrist free and slid his hand through the fly front of Lucas's drawers.

Lucas jolted, as if his touch stung.

Tom wrapped his fingers around hot, hard flesh. "I want to suck you again," he whispered in Lucas's ear.

"No . . ." Lucas's voice strangled in a groan as Tom squeezed.

"Why not?" Tom said.

Lucas caught his breath, and groaned again deep in his chest, and said hoarsely, "Because if anyone sees us, we'll be *hanged*."

"It's as dark as a coal-pit, Lu. No one's going to see us."

Lucas's breath was wheezing. "Someone could."

"I can't even see you, Lu." He pressed his mouth to Lucas's earlobe, to his cheek, to his lips, while his hands were busy with Lucas's buttons. "And if I can't see you, no one else can." He freed Lucas's cock from the drawers, took it in his hand again, stroked its length.

Lucas trembled, and groaned breathlessly, and said, "Tom, we *can't*—"

"It's all right, Lu," Tom said, and he kissed Lucas again, a longer kiss this time, reassuring him, and then he knelt and took Lucas's cock in his mouth.

Lucas inhaled sharply, a sound like a sob. His fingers

buried themselves in Tom's hair, not pushing him away, not pulling him closer, just holding him.

Tom let that hot, smooth, blunt head rest on his tongue for a moment. Pleasure hummed in his throat. No taste in the world could possibly be as exhilarating as this. He ran his tongue over the contours, tracing the slit, following the ridge between head and shaft.

Lucas groaned, and trembled.

Tom took more of Lucas's cock into his mouth and sucked hard.

Lucas grunted as if he'd been kicked in the stomach. His hips bucked.

Tom laughed around Lucas's cock, took a good grip on the shaft with one hand, and sucked a second time, even harder.

He set a fast rhythm. There were times when slow was good and times when fast was good, and here, in a public mews in the middle of London, fast was definitely best.

Lucas was gasping for breath, and each gasp had a moan in it. His fingers clenched in Tom's hair—and then his body shuddered and his cock jerked.

Tom stayed where he was for almost a minute, kneeling, reveling in the powerful intimacy of the moment: Lucas's fingers relaxed in his hair, Lucas's musky scent in his nostrils, Lucas's cock hot and spent in his mouth, the taste of Lucas's mettle on his tongue. *This isn't a dream; it's real.*

Finally, he gave a silent sigh and sat back on his heels. Lucas's fingers slid from his hair, Lucas's cock slid from his mouth.

Tom climbed to his feet. He fastened Lucas's drawers, fastened the pantaloons, tucked the shirt back in. Lucas was shaking. His breathing was low and ragged, almost as if he was weeping. Tom put his arms around him and held him tightly. *I love you, Lu.*

"Damn you," Lucas whispered hoarsely, and then he took a deep, hitching breath and shoved Tom away, pushing past him, heading for Avery Row.

Tom reached out blindly, caught Lucas's arm, and swung him back. "Don't tell me you didn't enjoy that, because we both know you damned well *did*."

"Fuck you," Lucas said, shrugging off his hand.

"You just did. Fuck me."

"This isn't funny! This isn't a joke!" There was real anguish in Lucas's voice. "We could be hanged!"

"Lu . . ."

"I'm not doing this. I *won't* do this!"

Tom caught Lucas's arm again and stepped close to him. "I almost died in Portugal," he said, in a low, fierce voice. "I am *not* walking away from this."

Lucas said nothing. He was tense, trembling.

Tom leaned close and kissed him, finding Lucas's cheek with his mouth.

Lucas turned his head away. "We can't do this," he said, sounding close to tears.

"We can. If we're careful." Tom kissed Lucas again, pressing his lips lightly to the taut plane of Lucas's cheek, and then released him and stepped back. "Good night, Lu."

Chapter Five

October 8th, 1808
London

LUCAS HEARD THE knock on the door, but paid no attention to it. He sat in his armchair, a book unread on his lap, his head in his hands, reliving that dreadful moment in the Brook Street Mews.

His strongest emotion was shame. Shame more intense than any he'd experienced in his life. *How could I have let him do it? How could I have enjoyed it?*

But however much he wished it hadn't happened, it had. He'd *allowed* it to happen—and now he had to deal with the consequences.

I can't see Tom ever again. He knew it—he was taking steps to ensure it—but the emotion he felt wasn't relief; it was despair. He and Tom had been best friends since their very first day at Eton. Nineteen years. Nearly twenty. How could he never see Tom again?

A key scraped in the keyhole. The door opened.

Lucas lifted his head. Smollet was back already? He turned in the chair—and saw Tom step into the entrance hall.

Panic kicked in Lucas's belly. He scrambled to his feet. "What are you doing here?"

Tom put the key back in his pocket. "Came to see you, muttonhead. Why else would I be here?"

"But it's morning." And then Lucas caught the significance of Tom's clothes. "You're not in uniform."

"Wellesley gave me some leave. Says he doesn't need me under his feet."

"But the inquiry—"

"They won't be taking testimony for at least another month." Tom halted in the middle of the sitting room. "We need to talk, Lu." He caught sight of the trunk, already corded. His eyebrows rose. "Going somewhere?"

"Whiteoaks," Lucas said. "Always do, this time of year." And then he shut his mouth and listened to his heartbeat thud in his ears.

Tom looked at him for several seconds, his gaze cool and assessing. "Running away?"

Lucas flushed—but didn't deny the charge. Yes, he was running away.

Tom pulled off his gloves and tossed them on the nearest table. "Look, Lu—"

"I don't want to discuss it," Lucas said firmly.

A faint glint of laughter lit Tom's eyes. "Chickenhearted, Lu?" He took off his hat and shrugged out of his greatcoat.

Lucas's panic scrambled up from his belly to his chest, where it squeezed his lungs. "I'm busy. I must ask you to leave."

The glint of laughter faded. Tom's expression became serious. "Is that what you truly want? For me to leave?"

Lucas looked away. "Yes."

For a long moment, there was silence. Lucas stared at the nearest bookcase, and felt the panic tight in his chest, and waited desperately for the sound of Tom picking up his great-coat. It didn't come.

"Then you'll have to throw me out, because I'm not leaving until we've talked about this."

Anger sparked in Lucas's breast. He swung his gaze back to Tom. "Damn it, these are *my* rooms!"

Tom shrugged. "So, throw me out."

Lucas clenched his fists and glared at him, torn between panic and anger.

Tom stared back, a bulldog expression on his face.

They both knew that if he wanted to, Lucas could throw Tom out. Tom was taller, but Lucas was brawnier—and he had a right hook that could floor an ox.

Tom's eyebrows lifted. "No? Let's talk, then."

He crossed to the fireplace—and Lucas suddenly knew how a hen felt when it was cornered by a fox. He felt a burst of panic and struck out wildly. Not a right hook, and not with his full body weight behind it, but enough of a punch that Tom reeled back a pace, tripped over the ottoman, and fell heavily.

Lucas took a horrified step forward—and forced himself to halt.

Tom pushed up on one elbow and gingerly touched his cheek. "What the devil was that for?"

"I asked you to leave," Lucas said stiffly. He felt sick to the pit of his belly. *I hit Tom.*

Tom climbed to his feet. "If you want me to leave, you're going to have to hit me harder than that."

Lucas clenched his hands again—and knew he couldn't hit Tom a second time.

Tom stepped over the ottoman. "Lucas, we *have* to talk."

Lucas retreated behind his armchair.

Tom halted, and put his eyebrows up. The glint of laughter lit his eyes again. "Why are you hiding behind that chair?"

"Because I won't be a sodomite!" Lucas said fiercely.

Tom blinked. "What?"

"You heard me. Get out of here."

"You think I'm going to bend you over a table and swive you, right now?" Tom's expression was affronted. "Christ, Lu! Who the devil do you think I am?"

"I don't think you'll do that," Lucas said gruffly. *I wouldn't let you.*

"Then why the deuce are you behind that chair?"

Lucas shifted his gaze back to the bookcase. "Because I don't want . . . what happened last night to happen again," he said, and felt shame heat his face.

Stiff, stilted seconds ticked past, and Tom didn't respond to this statement. The silence stretched. And stretched. Finally, Lucas risked a glance at him.

Tom no longer looked affronted. All the emotion was gone from his face. He stood on the rug in front of the fireplace, a bruise swelling along his left cheekbone, his gaze fixed on Lucas, his eyes narrow. That cool, green gaze was as sharp as a saber. *As if he's dissecting me.*

Lucas looked away. He came out from behind the armchair and crossed the sitting room, opened the door to the entrance hall. "Please leave."

Tom didn't move. "Why don't you want it to happen again, Lu?"

"Leave."

"Not until you tell me why." Tom took a step back, and

leaned against the mantelpiece, not nonchalant, but tense. "There's no one here to see us if we do it, so if that's not your reason, what is?"

Lucas tightened his grip on the door handle. "Leave, damn it."

"You enjoyed it last night—we both know you did—so why don't you want it?"

Shame flamed in Lucas's face again, even hotter this time. "Why? Because it's wrong, that's why!"

"Wrong?" Tom's lips thinned. He pushed away from the mantelpiece. "You mean it's disgusting and unnatural."

Lucas nodded stiffly.

Tom crossed the sitting room. "Is that how it felt to you? Disgusting and unnatural? Because that's not how it felt to me."

Lucas found himself unable to meet that hard, challenging gaze.

Tom halted in front of him. "Well, Lu? Did it?"

This was a Tom he didn't recognize, radiating tension, his good-humored face made of sharp angles. "Well?" Tom demanded again, thrusting out his chin, his eyes bright with anger. "Did it?"

No, it hadn't felt disgusting and unnatural, not while Tom had been kissing and touching him. It was only afterwards, when he'd come to his senses, his drawers hanging open and his cock soft and replete in Tom's mouth, that the full weight of horrified realization had struck him.

He'd accepted sexual intimacies from a man.

Accepted them, and *enjoyed* them.

"Answer me, damn you." Tom stepped so close that their bodies almost touched. "Did it feel disgusting last night?"

"Afterwards—"

"Fuck afterwards," Tom said. "Does *this* feel disgusting?" And he leaned in and kissed Lucas.

Lucas flinched, and raised his hands to shove Tom away—and then he gave a helpless sob in his throat and surrendered, opening his mouth to Tom.

Tom's kiss was fierce, angry, almost desperate. His fingers dug into Lucas's hair, holding him still, but Lucas didn't try to break free; he gripped the lapels of Tom's coat and kissed him back. Kissed him. Kissed him. It didn't feel disgusting or unnatural. It felt as if he'd been living his whole life for this moment: Tom's mouth devouring his, Tom's body pressed close.

Tom's fingers relaxed in Lucas's hair, cradling his skull. The kiss became comfort, not confrontation. Their mouths moved more slowly—long, deep, tender kisses. Kisses that turned Lucas inside out. Kisses that made him feel as if his soul had taken wings and was flying.

Finally, Tom turned his head away and rested his cheek against Lucas's.

They stood holding each other, panting. Lucas felt Tom's hands cupping his skull, felt Tom's long, lean body pressed close, felt Tom's warm breath on his cheek. Now that they were no longer kissing, the panic returned, fluttering in his chest. "I won't be a sodomite," he whispered.

"I'm not asking you to be one, Lu. On my word of honor, I'll never ask that of you." Tom's fingers moved in Lucas's hair, stroking gently. "All I'm asking is that you let me do what I did last night."

Lucas flinched inwardly. The flutter of panic became stronger.

Perhaps Tom sensed that internal flinch, for he pressed his mouth lightly to Lucas's cheek. "But only if you can bring yourself to allow it. And only on the understanding that you owe me nothing in return."

Lucas squeezed his eyes shut, and felt the panic expand inside him. Memory of the Brook Street Mews was vivid in his mind. From the moment Tom had touched his cock, he'd been helpless to resist. Reasoning had shut down. His awareness of the world had narrowed to one thing: pleasure. Pleasure so intense that a dozen carriages could have driven past and he wouldn't have noticed. It was only afterwards that his brain had resumed working. The pleasure had snuffed instantly. Other emotions had taken its place: horror, shame, panic.

Those three emotions were still with him—and accompanying them, tightly entwined, inseparable from them, was an ache of longing. Longing deep in his bones. He wanted what Tom was offering. Wanted the heart-stopping intimacy, wanted the ecstasy, and most of all, just wanted Tom. Tom with him. Tom touching him. Tom.

"Nothing more than last night. I swear it, Lu."

Lucas wrestled with the shame and horror and panic and the bone-deep ache of his longing for Tom. *I should push him away.* But his heart was beating Tom's name again: *Tom, Tom, Tom.*

"Please, Lu."

Lucas gave in to the ache. "If . . . if it's what you want." On the heels of those words, came a spurt of panic. *Oh, God, did I just say that?*

Tom exhaled, a sound like a sigh. "Thank you." He pressed a kiss to Lucas's mouth. One hand strayed down to Lucas's waistband.

"Not now," Lucas said, the panic spiking in his chest. He drew sharply back.

Tom looked at him for a moment, somberly, and then gave a small, wry, lopsided smile. "Not if you don't want to."

Lucas flushed, and looked away. "Smollet could return."

Tom reached out and touched Lucas's hair again lightly. "Trust me, Lu. I'm not going to ruin us, or get us hanged."

You can't promise that. Lucas turned his head and looked at Tom—the angular face, the unruly black hair, the sooty lashes, the mobile mouth. The drumbeat of Tom's name grew louder in his head. *Tom, Tom, Tom.* He dragged his gaze from Tom's mouth and fastened it instead on the swelling bruise beneath Tom's left eye. "I'm sorry I hit you."

"I'm sorry I made you feel you had to." Tom cupped the back of Lucas's head in one hand again and leaned in and kissed him—fleeting, gentle—and then put his arms around Lucas and hugged him. "I'm coming to Whiteoaks with you."

God, it felt good to have Tom hold him. Lucas wanted to lean into that embrace. He held himself rigid. "The inquiry—"

"Won't start for weeks. Wellesley's not even sure he'll need my testimony. Burghersh will speak for him, and Torrens. They have higher rank than me."

"You're an earl's son."

Tom laughed softly in his ear. "Not that kind of rank, stoopid." His hug tightened.

Lucas gave in, and let himself lean into Tom.

"And if it turns out Wellesley does need me, I can post back. It's only Wiltshire, after all."

Lucas closed his eyes and rested his forehead on Tom's shoulder, and inexplicably felt like crying.

"Your brother's got two hundred bedrooms. I doubt he'd begrudge me one."

"Seventy-six bedrooms," Lucas said, into Tom's shoulder. "Of course he wouldn't mind. You're one of the family."

Tom tightened his grip. "I'm coming. All right?"

Lucas nodded, and squeezed his eyes shut. *Don't ever stop*

holding me. And then he took a deep breath and pushed away from Tom. "We're leaving at one. Want to get to Reading by dark."

"One?" Tom glanced at the corded trunk, and then back at him. "You *were* running away, weren't you?"

"Yes," Lucas admitted. *And perhaps it would be better for us both if I still did.*

Chapter Six

SMOLLET LEFT LONDON at one o'clock, in a post-chaise, with Lucas's trunk and Tom's portmanteau, but it was closer to two by the time Lucas climbed into his curricle. He was able to ignore Tom's proximity while he threaded his way through the London traffic, but once they came out into the countryside, it became impossible. He was intensely aware of Tom seated alongside him, intensely aware that their thighs almost touched. The beat began again, in his head, in his blood: *Tom, Tom.*

Tom didn't try to talk. He sat alongside Lucas, relaxed, slouching slightly.

Silences between them had always been comfortable before, but this silence wasn't comfortable—it was taut with expectancy. The air seemed to crackle, as if lightning had struck nearby. Lucas found himself sweating slightly. He wasn't sure why—the afternoon was edging from chilly towards freezing—but sweat prickled on his skin. Fear? Anticipation?

They didn't reach Reading. Didn't even come close. Three

hours out of London, it started to rain, sparse, fat drops that struck the curricle with audible *splats*.

He glanced at Tom.

Tom was still slouching, his thigh still almost touching Lucas's. "Going to get worse. Look at that sky."

I know.

"Want to put the hood up, or stop at the next inn for the night?"

Lucas hesitated. "What would you prefer?"

"I'd rather not get wet."

"The hood——"

"The wind's in our faces; the hood won't help much." Tom's glance was appraising. "But we can try for Reading if you like. We won't melt."

Ordinarily, he'd stop at the nearest inn. Smollet wouldn't worry if they failed to reach Reading; he'd look at the sky and guess they'd halted early. But Lucas had the feeling that stopping now would be dangerous. Very dangerous.

"Let's see how far we can get," he said, determined to push through to Reading and Smollet and safety. But half a mile later, the skies opened, and even with the hood up, bitter rain swept into their faces, and when they rounded a bend and saw a country tavern, small and old and half-timbered, with light glowing in the tiny-paned windows, he didn't hesitate at all, but turned the curricle into the yard.

THE INN WAS CALLED the White Hart, and it was more used to farm laborers wearing smocks and hobnailed brogues than to gentry. The whitewash was peeling and the furniture had seen better days, but despite those things the White Hart was warm and cozy and welcoming.

The innkeeper gave them two rooms up under the eaves and begged their pardon that he had no private parlor, but Lucas was relieved. No private parlor meant no time alone with Tom.

They ate mutton pie in the taproom, rubbing shoulders with farmers and a blacksmith and two carters who'd taken refuge from the rain.

Tom pushed his plate away with a contented sigh. "Best meal I've had in a long time." He drained his tankard, and fished in his pocket for his sketchbook and pencil.

Lucas slowly finished his ale. The taproom was warm and noisy, Tom's attention was on his sketches—eyes slightly narrowed, pencil moving swiftly—but tension was still tight between them, a silent hiss in the air.

Lucas pushed his plate away, and stood. "I'm off to bed."

Tom looked up sharply.

Lucas read the question in his eyes—and found himself unable to breathe. His balls tightened. Panic and craving knotted together in his belly.

The panic won.

"Stay down here," Lucas said. "Lots of faces for you to sketch. I'll, uh, see you in the morning." And then he fled the taproom.

THEY'D EACH BROUGHT a small valise, stowed in the empty groom's seat. Lucas locked his door, found a nightshirt, and climbed into bed—and didn't sleep. He lay awake listening to the rain, thinking about what he'd seen on Tom's face.

Part of him wanted to go next door to Tom's bedchamber and apologize, to let Tom kiss him. And part of him wanted to get dressed and creep down the back stairs, harness the horses to the curricle and run away. This was the middle ground, hiding in his room.

There is no right path through this. Whatever choice I make will be wrong. Running away was wrong. Hiding was wrong. Being intimate with Tom was wrong.

Lucas's chest grew tight. Sleep receded still further. He found himself longing for the bitter taste of laudanum, for the retreat from reality it offered. But that, too, would be wrong.

Finally, he sat up, lit a candle, and rummaged in the valise for his book.

LUCAS FELL ASLEEP close to dawn and woke mid-morning to the sound of rain. He climbed out of bed and opened the shutters. Yes, rain. He sighed, and leaned his hands on the windowsill, and felt as gray as the sky.

Tom was already in the taproom, eating his way through a plate of ham and eggs. His greeting was cheerful, as if they'd parted on good terms, but Lucas could still remember the way Tom's face had stiffened last night, the way the bright expectancy had extinguished in his eyes.

Whatever choice I make will be wrong.

Lucas pulled out a chair and returned Tom's greeting, but there was tension in his shoulders, tension in the back of his neck.

A plate of fried ham and eggs and a tankard of ale made him feel slightly less gray, but did nothing for his tension; the longer he sat next to Tom, the more aware of him he was— and the tighter his muscles became.

"Chess?" Tom said. "There's a set in one of the cupboards."

Lucas shrugged stiffly. "Why not?"

They pushed aside their plates and played chess. Usually they were evenly matched, but this morning Lucas found himself unable to concentrate. Tom beat him quickly, twice.

"You all right?" Tom said, when Lucas lost for the second time.

"Bit tired," Lucas admitted. "Didn't sleep too well."

"You want to stop?"

"No." At least the chess disguised the awkward constraint between them.

They were halfway through a third game—and Lucas was losing again—when the innkeeper's wife bustled in with a mop and a bucket of water.

"Want to finish this game?" Tom said diffidently. "There's a table and chairs in my room."

Lucas hesitated. He thought of his half-read book—and then he remembered the hurt on Tom's face last night. "Why not?" But once they were upstairs in Tom's room, a fire burning in the grate, he regretted his decision. This was too cozy, too intimate, too private.

He lost the third game in six moves. "Another game?" Tom said.

Lucas picked up a pawn and turned it over in his fingers, the movements sharp, almost agitated. "No point, is there?" He turned the pawn over again, *flick, flick,* avoiding Tom's gaze. "Not much of a game for you. Boring."

Tom reached out and caught his hand, stilling the movement. "Lu, relax. I told you, I won't do anything you don't want."

Lucas gripped the pawn tightly. His heartbeat grew loud in his ears: *Tom, Tom, Tom.*

He lifted his gaze—and found that he couldn't look away from those green, bright eyes. The crackling tension intensified. The air felt charged with expectancy. The back of his neck was tight, his shoulders were tight, his chest was tight—and Tom's fingers burned on his skin.

They stared at each other for a long moment, and then Tom released his hand. "You won't be a sodomite, Lu. I promise."

Lucas tried to swallow, but his throat was too constricted.

Tom pushed back his chair and stood slowly, came around the table slowly, bent slowly, kissed him slowly—a gentle kiss, a kiss that demanded nothing.

Lucas's breath caught in his throat in a sound close to a sob.

Tom kissed him again, and whispered against his mouth, "Relax, Lu."

Relax? How could he relax when craving was tying his stomach in knots, and his lungs had clenched in his chest, and his balls were painfully tight?

"Relax," Tom whispered again, against his lips—and Lucas gave in to the craving and kissed him back, desperately, urgently.

Tom made a sound—sigh? groan?—and deepened the kiss, no longer gentle, but insistent.

Lucas dropped the pawn. He reached out and gripped Tom and hauled him closer, and kissed him—kissed him —kissed him.

He didn't release Tom until they were both panting heavily.

Tom straightened. His face was flushed, his green eyes even brighter than usual. "The bed," he said.

Lucas flinched.

"Nothing more than the mews, stoopid. But we may as well be comfortable."

Lucas looked down at the hard floor and imagined Tom

kneeling there. Heat flooded his groin—and shame flushed his face. "All right," he managed to say.

Tom stepped back.

Lucas stood, a jerky movement. "The door—"

Tom crossed to the door, turned the key, and came back to the table. "Come on, Lu."

Lucas's panic surged—but he let Tom take him by the wrist and draw him across to the bed. His legs were stiff with trepidation and his cock was stiffening, too.

"Tailcoat off," Tom said. "And those boots. And your neck-cloth, too."

"But—"

"Tailcoat, boots, and neckcloth," Tom said firmly, and reached up and unwound his own neckcloth.

Lucas fumbled his way out of his tailcoat. The anticipation and trepidation were building. His fingers trembled. It took him three tries to get the neckcloth off.

"Sit," Tom said. "I'll pull your boots off."

Lucas hesitated, and sat on the very edge of the bed. He had a sharp burst of memory: the night of his birthday, Tom pulling off his boots, unbuttoning his breeches, sucking his cock.

Tom removed the top boots. "And your waistcoat, too. Don't want to crease it."

Lucas groped for the buttons, struggling to get them out of the buttonholes. To his mortification, his cock was as rigid as it had ever been, tenting his breeches. He couldn't meet Tom's eyes.

"I'll do it." Tom bent and undid the buttons, peeled him swiftly out of the waistcoat, then stepped back.

Lucas reluctantly looked at him. God, Tom was beautiful, tall and lean in his shirt-sleeves and breeches and stockings. His gaze skidded down to Tom's groin, and hastily away—but not before he'd seen the hard outline pressed against the fabric.

He felt his face flush hotly. His heart began to beat even faster.

Tom stepped close again. "Lie down, Lu."

Panic lurched in Lucas's chest.

"Lie down," Tom said, a second time, and he pushed Lucas back on the bed, gently but firmly.

Lucas's stomach was tight, his lungs were tight, every muscle in his body was tight. *Oh, God,* a panicked voice said, at the back of his head.

The mattress dipped as Tom sat down. Lucas's heart beat even faster, so fast it surely must burst. He felt the same mix of emotions he'd felt in the Brook Street Mews: shame, panic— and craving.

"Relax, Lu." Tom stretched out alongside him and gathered him in his arms and kissed him softly, lightly, tenderly. "Relax."

Lucas's heart stopped galloping quite so fast. It became slightly easier to breathe.

They kissed for several minutes, their mouths gentle against each other. Finally, Tom pulled back. "Better?" He stroked a strand of hair from Lucas's brow.

Lucas nodded mutely.

"Good." Tom smiled, and sat up.

Lucas stared up at the bedhangings. *Oh, God.* The panic and the craving came surging back. He lay rigid with shame, every muscle taut, while Tom unbuttoned his breeches and pushed the plackets aside, while he unbuttoned his drawers. *Oh, God.*

He flinched when Tom touched his aching cock.

Tom laughed softly. "Relax, Lu."

Relax? How could he relax when Tom was gripping him

like that? He flinched a second time when Tom lightly blew, and a third time when he licked, his tongue warm and velvety.

When Tom had done this in the darkness of the Brook Street Mews, he'd done it fast; here, on the bed, he did it slowly—excruciatingly slowly—licking his way down Lucas's cock and back up again, tasting every inch of skin, licking, licking, licking.

Lucas lay with his eyes squeezed shut, panting, trembling, listening to the deafening beat of Tom's name in his head. When Tom finally took his cock into his mouth and sucked, Lucas's hips bucked helplessly.

Tom laughed, and sucked again.

Lucas groaned.

Time twisted in on itself. This was exquisite, agonizing torture: Tom's tight, gripping hand, Tom's hot, hot mouth. Pressure built inside him, built and built and built until it felt as if his skin would rupture—and then he did rupture, splintering into a thousand pieces, pleasure bursting through him in great jolts, and he bucked and cried out, a breathless, strangled sound.

It took nearly a minute for the spasms to stop.

Lucas lay trembling, panting, dazed. Dimly, he was aware of Tom coming to lie on the bed alongside him.

Finally he inhaled a deep, shuddering breath. "Jesus." His voice was hoarse.

"Good, huh?" Tom's voice was smug, and when Lucas turned his head to look at him, his expression was smug, too.

Tom grinned, and stretched like a satisfied cat, and reached out and stroked Lucas's hair.

They lay there in silence, while the tingling pleasure slowly faded. Shame took its place, like a tide creeping in. Shame, and a new emotion: guilt. Here he lay, his cock warm and sated, and he wasn't going to offer Tom an intimacy in return.

Tom didn't expect anything from him—he'd *said* he didn't expect anything—but that didn't make it any less wrong.

Lucas lay on the bed, while the tide of shame and guilt crept higher.

I won't do anything you don't want, Tom had said, and Lucas knew what he didn't want, knew down to the marrow of his bones what he *didn't* want—but he didn't have the same certainty about what he did want.

Did he want to touch Tom the way Tom had touched him? Perhaps even taste him?

He thought the answer might be *Yes,* and that brought a surge of panic. *I can't.* It was too much, too soon, too daunting.

Tom wasn't afraid. He made it seem easy, the easiest thing in the world, as if it took no courage at all to kneel at another man's feet and take his cock in one's mouth.

The moment of insight came suddenly: *Tom's done this with someone else.*

Lucas felt a stab of jealousy so intense it was almost anger. He turned his head and looked at Tom. "You've done this before, haven't you?"

Chapter Seven

TOM'S MUSCLES TENSED SLIGHTLY. "What? You mean sex? Of course I have."

"I mean sex with a man."

"Uh . . ." *Should I tell him the truth?* "Yes," Tom said. "Once. I mean, not one time, but one man."

Tom tried to decipher Lucas's expression. Revulsion? Censure?

"Who was he?"

Jealousy. That was the expression on Lucas's face: jealousy.

Tom relaxed. He stroked Lucas's hair, drawing the golden strands slowly through his fingers. Arousal pulsed in his blood. His cock was taut and hot and aching. Not a painful ache, a pleasurable ache. "He was one of my commanding officers."

Lucas's forehead furrowed in a fierce frown. "One of your superiors took advantage of you?"

"Advantage?" Tom laughed. "No. It just happened." And then he thought about this statement and amended it slightly.

"Maybe he did seduce me, but only once he knew I wanted it."

Lucas was still frowning severely.

"It was . . ." Lord. How to describe what had happened? "He was a colonel, and he took me as his aide-de-camp, and he was . . . He was one of the best soldiers I've ever met. He was absolutely fair, and he had a sharp mind, and he was brave and . . . and *staunch*—someone you could always rely on, you know?—and he had this way of telling jokes, when you least expected it, and . . . I fell a little in love with him. Which I hadn't expected."

He hesitated. How much of the truth would Lucas be willing to hear? *But I didn't love Colonel Armagh nearly as much as I love you.* He bit the words back, and said, "I tried to hide it, but one evening we were in his quarters and we'd been drinking—there was some celebration or other, I don't remember what—and we were both a bit top-heavy, and he was pointing something out on the map, leaning over me, and there was this moment when I wanted to kiss him—when I almost *did* kiss him—just a couple of seconds—and I made an excuse and got out of there as fast as I could. I was in a cold sweat all night, afraid he'd noticed, but the next day he treated me the same as always—God, that was a relief!—except that he *had* noticed, and a week or so later he brought out the brandy, and said he'd had good news from home, and we had a drink, and another one, and . . . and then he leaned over me again, his face this close to mine—" He held his hands half a foot apart. "And I wanted to kiss him—and . . . and then *he* kissed *me*."

And the world had frozen for a moment.

Tom's throat tightened in memory. "It was the most incredible kiss I'd ever had." *Until I kissed you.* "The surprise, I guess, and all the months I'd been wanting him, and the fact that it was dangerous. Forbidden." He'd returned Colonel

Armagh's kiss, dizzy with shock, dizzy with exhilaration. "He kissed me half-senseless, and then he got down on his knees and . . ." Tom's throat tightened still further. His cock tightened, too. He shivered at the memory: Armagh unbuttoning his breeches, Armagh sucking him. "It was the best sex I've ever had. I came so hard I just about fainted."

Lucas was staring at him, his mouth thin and tight, a sharp crease between his eyebrows—an expression Tom interpreted as jealousy.

"After that, we were lovers. Eight months. Then his brother died, and he inherited a baronetcy, so he sold out and came home."

"Will you see him while you're here?" Lucas asked stiffly.

Tom shook his head. "He's married. Last I heard, his wife was pregnant."

"Married?" The crease between Lucas's eyebrows deepened.

"He's got a title and an estate now; got to have an heir."

"But . . . but he's a back door usher!"

"Oh, Armagh likes women well enough. He just likes men, too." He paused, and looked at Lucas's face. *How much should I tell him?* "And he's not really a back door usher. He'd rather roger a woman than a man. He used to say that women were more fun for swiving, but for oral congress, he preferred men, because men knew their way around a cock better."

Lucas's frown became quite ferocious. "He was using you."

"What?" Where had Lucas got that notion from? Tom reviewed his last words. "You think he trained me up so he'd have a man to suck him? Of course, he didn't! Armagh always gave as good as he got."

For some reason, that made Lucas flinch.

"He wasn't using me, Lu. He never forced me to do anything I didn't want to do."

49

Lucas looked unconvinced.

"He wasn't a dirty old colonel exploiting an aide," Tom said, growing annoyed. "He's only forty, and dashed good-looking, and clever and funny and brave, and I was *in love* with him."

That made Lucas flinch again, but Tom was too cross to care. "And it was *good*. It wasn't filthy or disgusting. It was *good*." He took a deep breath, caught his temper, and exhaled slowly. "Armagh wasn't using me. Trust me, Lu: he wasn't."

"Was he in love with you?" Lucas said stiffly.

"A bit. About as much as I was with him."

Lucas's lips tightened. "Did you . . . you know . . . do it with him?"

Tom didn't pretend to misunderstand. "Once. Armagh said I needed to know whether I liked it or not, and it was safer to do it with him than with some molly boy in a backstreet alley. So I did." He shrugged. "I didn't like it. Armagh was right: it's more fun to swive a woman. And as for *being* swived . . . it was . . ." He tried to find the words to describe the sense of invasion, of powerlessness. "It made me wonder what women think about sex, whether they actually *like* it."

He studied Lucas's face, and saw the censure there. *Fuck it, I'm not going to feel ashamed.* "It wasn't awful—although it did hurt a bit—but I felt as if . . . as if I had no control. I felt . . . I don't know, helpless. I guess some fellows like that feeling, but I don't. I was glad Armagh didn't want to do it again." *Listen to me, Lu.* "So, you see, when I say I'll never ask you to be a back door usher, I mean it."

Lucas broke their eye contact.

Tom stared at him in frustration. The warm sense of intimacy between them was gone. His hot, taut, aching arousal had extinguished. *Damn* Lucas for being so narrow-minded. "So that's my sordid past," he said, trying to keep his voice light and cheerful. "I've had sex with half a hundred women, and one man. Two, counting you. What about you?"

A dull flush crept along Lucas's cheekbones. He sat up and buttoned his drawers.

Tom sat up, too. "How many, Lu?"

Lucas ignored him, and fastened his breeches.

"What?" Tom said. A hard note crept into his voice. "It's all right for you to ask me who I've swived, but not for me to ask you?"

Lucas turned his head and looked at him. "No one," he said flatly. "All right? No one."

"What?"

"You heard me." Lucas climbed off the bed. His face was tight again, his lips compressed, his movements jerky.

Tom caught his wrist and yanked him back down to sit. "What the devil do you mean no one? I was *there* the first time you did it. I *saw* you go up the stairs. You and that highflyer you'd chosen."

Lucas turned his head and looked at him. He didn't say anything. He didn't need to; his expression said it for him— bleak, bitter, ashamed.

Tom released his grip on Lucas's wrist. "But I *saw* you go up the stairs."

Lucas turned his head away. "Well, you didn't see me in the bedroom, did you? I might as well have been a eunuch."

"But . . . you never said anything."

"Would *you* have?" Lucas looked down at his hands, and clenched them together. "She was pretty, I could see that, but I just . . . I just couldn't . . . it just didn't work."

"Jesus," Tom said. "So you've never . . . ?"

Lucas clenched his hands until the knuckles whitened. "I've tried twice since, and it doesn't work. I can't *do* it."

"You did it with me just fine," Tom said.

Lucas grimaced, and stared down at his fists.

"What about, um, tossing off? Can you . . . ?"

Lucas flushed crimson. He averted his head and gave a stiff nod.

So, Lucas could have sex with his own hand, but not with a woman.

Tom tried to imagine what it would be like to select a courtesan, to strip naked in front of her, and be unable to perform. He winced inwardly.

The lightskirt wouldn't have laughed at Lucas; she'd have tried to coax him to arousal—sex was her trade after all, and she'd have *wanted* Lucas for a customer. Any whore would. Among a clientele of paunchy, middle-aged men, Lucas would stand out like a gift from the gods. His golden good looks, his physique, his wealth . . . whores would line up for his patronage. The three women he'd selected wouldn't have given up easily. They'd have fondled his balls, teased his cock, stroked and licked and sucked and nibbled—until finally they admitted defeat—and Lucas would have dressed again, mortified and humiliated.

No wonder he didn't try a fourth time.

Tom felt slightly sick. Sick with guilt. All these years he'd been jumping in and out of women's beds, and Lucas had been alone and celibate and thinking there was something was wrong with him—and he hadn't noticed. "Christ, Lu, you should have *said* something." He hooked his arm around Lucas's neck, pulled him close, kissed his cheek.

"How could I?" Lucas said, and he sounded close to tears.

Tom tightened his grip. *He must have been very lonely. Very unhappy.* "I'm sorry. I should have noticed."

Lucas didn't relax against him; he stayed stiff, tense, miserable, his head slightly averted. "You weren't here most of the time."

No, he'd been off soldiering, while Lucas had been back in England, without any lovers, without a best friend—and for the past sixteen months, without a twin sister.

Tom's sense of guilt increased sharply. "I'm sorry," he said again. He remembered their first kiss, rough and fierce and clumsy. "In the mews . . . was that the first time you've kissed someone?"

Lucas nodded, and inhaled a hitching breath, and rubbed his face roughly.

He's almost crying.

"You do it very well," Tom said, pressing his mouth to Lucas's cheek again.

"No, I don't," Lucas whispered.

"Yes, you do—better than Colonel Armagh, and I used to think no one could be better than him."

Lucas shook his head.

"But if you disagree, we can practice some more." He laid his lips to Lucas's cheek a third time. *I love you, Lu.* "Come on, Lu, make up for lost time . . ."

Lucas inhaled another hitching breath.

"Take pity on a poor soldier . . ." Tom said, in a quavering voice.

Lucas huffed a faint laugh, and then sighed. Some of the tension drained from him.

Tom kissed the very corner of Lucas's mouth. After a pause, Lucas turned his head and kissed Tom back, hesitantly, almost shyly.

They kissed sitting up, and then, after several minutes, Tom drew Lucas down to lie on the bed again. He kept the kisses light; this wasn't about sex, this was about reassurance and comfort. Slow, tender kisses. And he could scarcely believe that Lucas had never kissed anyone else; he was so *good* at it.

He told Lucas that, when they came up for air. "You're *way* better than Armagh."

Lucas blushed, and shook his head.

Tom leaned in and caught Lucas's lower lip between his teeth, nipped lightly, nipped a second time, then turned his attention to Lucas's throat, nibbling his way downwards, pushing the collar aside, tasting the salt on Lucas's skin with his tongue, testing his shoulder muscles lightly with his teeth. He opened the buttons of Lucas's shirt, found one of his nipples, pinched it.

Lucas inhaled a short, sharp breath.

Tom laughed. "Like that?" he asked, and pinched again.

Lucas groaned low in his throat. "Yes."

Tom spent some time on Lucas's nipples, licking, biting, sucking, teasing. Each twitch Lucas made, each stifled moan, stoked Tom's own arousal. It was always a powerful experience to give pleasure to someone and this time it was more powerful than it had ever been before, because it was Lucas—Lucas whom he'd loved for years but not dared to touch.

Finally, he abandoned Lucas's nipples and returned to his mouth. This time their kisses were urgent, fierce. They gripped each other close, mouths clashing, and then Tom found himself on his back and Lucas was kissing his throat roughly, licking and nipping, nothing gentle or leisurely about it at all—hungry, burning kisses—and then Lucas dug his strong teeth into the curve where Tom's neck met his shoulder, and Tom jackknifed on the bed, pleasure searing from his scalp all the way to the soles of his feet.

Lucas stopped biting. "Did I hurt you?"

"Christ, no," Tom said hoarsely. "Do it again."

Lucas hesitated, and then obeyed, finding the muscle, biting.

Pleasure jolted through Tom again. A strangled sound

came from his mouth. His cock gave a huge surge. *I'm going to spill in my breeches.* "Stop," he said frantically, and Lucas did.

Tom sat up hastily. "Sorry," he said, unbuttoning his breeches with fumbling speed. "Just need to take care of this." He practically tore the buttons off his drawers. His cock lunged out, deep red, straining. Tom grabbed it and pinched hard beneath the head.

His eyes winced shut. He pinched even harder.

His urgent arousal slowly dwindled to more manageable levels. He found himself able to breathe again, able to open his eyes.

Lucas was staring at him.

"Sorry," Tom said, flushing. "Just about spilled all over myself."

Lucas didn't say anything. Tom tried to decipher his expression. Shock? Revulsion?

Great, he told himself. *Just when things were going so well you've managed to disgust him.* He shoved his cock inside his drawers— still hard, but not in imminent danger of disgracing him.

"No," Lucas said.

Tom stopped, and looked at him. "You want to see me?"

Lucas blushed scarlet and didn't meet his eyes.

Tom revised his assessment of Lucas's expression. Not shock or revulsion, but curiosity.

He stopped trying to cram his cock into his drawers. He opened the plackets wider and let Lucas look at him.

Chapter Eight

LUCAS'S BREATH SEEMED to choke in his throat. He felt slightly light-headed. The beat became louder in his ears: *Tom, Tom, Tom.*

Tom was quite different from him. Not just the black hair at his groin, but the shape of his balls, the shape of his cock. His own balls were round; Tom's were oval. Tom's cock was as long as his, but not as thick and its angle was different, jutting upwards rather than outwards. Its color was a deeper shade than his own cock ever achieved, berry red rather than salmon pink, and the crest was conical rather than blunt, shaped like an ancient Greek helmet. *Corinthian,* a little voice said—irrelevantly—in his head.

Lucas's throat choked even tighter. He swallowed and struggled to breathe—and felt craving clench in his belly.

He wanted to touch Tom's cock, wanted to feel the silky skin, the hard muscle, the heat.

He could see the slit clearly—and see the bead of clear liquid oozing from it.

The craving became stronger.

Lucas jerked his gaze from Tom's cock, and looked at Tom's eyes instead.

Tom was staring at him. "Want to touch it?"

Lucas swallowed. Vaguely, dimly, at the very back of his mind, he was aware of panic; but foremost was craving. Yes, he wanted to touch Tom's cock.

He swallowed again, tried to breathe, and gave a tiny, stiff, ashamed nod.

Tom made a *help yourself* gesture and said, "Be my guest."

A lump grew in Lucas's throat. He had to swallow twice this time. Slowly, he reached out. The drumbeat of Tom's name was loud in his ears and beneath it was a faint whine of panic—and then he touched that ruddy helmet, and the whine of panic died and the drumbeat became deafeningly loud: *Tom, Tom, Tom.*

Lucas inhaled a shallow breath and slowly traced the contours with his fingertips, following the helmet-like rim, catching the bead of moisture with his thumb, smoothing it over sleek, burning hot skin. When he'd thoroughly explored the crest he slid his hand lower and wrapped his fingers around the strong shaft. Tom's cock seemed to pulse in time with the drumbeat in his head. He glanced at Tom's face—and discovered that Tom wasn't watching his hand; he was staring intently at his face.

Lucas felt himself blush hotly. He looked back down at Tom's cock, red and straining in his hand, and saw another bead of moisture leak from the slit. *He's almost ready to climax.*

His craving intensified, clenching tightly in his belly. At the back of his brain, he was aware he should be horrified—but the craving was too fierce. Lucas experimentally stroked his hand down that hot, throbbing shaft and back up. Once. Twice. He glanced at Tom's face and did it a third time—

down, then up—and watched Tom tremble and catch his breath.

Lucas gripped more tightly and picked up speed. *This* was power: pumping Tom like this, making him gasp and shudder, making him lose control.

Tom reached out and caught his hand, stopping him.

Lucas looked at him, his mouth open to protest—and the words dried on his tongue. Such hot, hot eyes.

"You're hard again," Tom said hoarsely. "I can see it in your face."

Lucas didn't need to ask what that looked like; he could see for himself: the hectic flush along Tom's cheekbones, the dilated pupils.

Tom fumbled at Lucas's waistband. "We'll do this together."

Lucas held his breath while Tom unbuttoned the breeches, unbuttoned the drawers. His cock lunged out, thick and blunt-tipped, eager for Tom's hand.

Tom captured it, wrapped his fingers tightly around it.

Lucas's breath strangled in his throat. He groaned. His gaze jerked to Tom's face—and was caught.

Time seemed to slow, almost to stop. Never had he experienced a moment of such profound, heart-stopping intimacy: his cock in Tom's hand, Tom's cock in his hand, and Tom's eyes, hot and dark, staring into his soul.

The drumbeat in Lucas's head became so loud that it felt as if his skull would explode—and then Tom looked down at their hands, and Lucas was able to breathe again. He inhaled raggedly.

Tom tightened his grip and pumped once, hard.

Pleasure jolted through Lucas. His eyes squeezed shut. *Jesus.*

"Lie down, Lu."

Tom had to say it twice before the words penetrated the fog of arousal. "Lie down, Lu. It's better."

Lucas obeyed, and Tom was right: it *was* better, stretched out on the bed. *He's done this before, with that damned colonel of his.* But there was no space in his head for jealousy, not now, not while they were stroking and squeezing each other, pumping each other, and his heart was galloping, and he was hot enough to burst into flame.

"Lu, let go," Tom said breathlessly. "I'll do us both together." He peeled Lucas's fingers open and took them both in one grip. Their cocks pressed together, hot and slick and taut and throbbing.

Lucas's heart kicked in his chest. His balls tightened painfully. Breath hissed between his teeth.

"Like that?" Tom said.

Lucas opened his mouth to say *Yes,* but only an inarticulate groan came out.

Tom laughed, and leaned closer, until his mouth touched Lucas's. "Kiss me."

Lucas did, fierce, bruising kisses, his fingers buried deep in Tom's hair, while their cocks clashed in Tom's hand and their bodies strove against each other. *Not long. Not long now.*

Tom's hand moved faster, the kisses became more frantic, and then the moment came—a vertiginous orgasm, like plunging over a cliff—and they bucked against each other for endless, endless, endless seconds.

Finally, the spasms faded. Lucas lay panting and exhausted, half-dazed.

Tom released their cocks, and stretched lazily. His eyes were dark and drowsy and his lips looked almost bruised, bee-stung.

If Tom's lips looked almost bruised, his left cheek definitely *was* bruised.

Lucas felt a sharp pang of remorse. He reached out and touched Tom's cheekbone, traced that purple mark. "I'm sorry I hit you."

"That? Lord, it's nothing." Tom smiled sleepily, and pulled Lucas close and hugged him.

Lucas pressed his face into Tom's shoulder. The drumbeat in his head was a slow, low beat: *Tom, Tom.*

They lay silently together, while the fire mumbled in the grate and rain pattered against the windowpanes. Lucas felt Tom's arms around him and listened to Tom's quiet breathing and knew that this was the most purely happy moment of his life.

WHEN LUCAS WOKE, Tom was sitting by the fire, a large sketchbook propped on his knees. Lucas stretched and yawned and rubbed his face. "What're you drawing?"

"You."

He yawned again, and buttoned his drawers and breeches, and climbed off the bed. "Lemme see."

Tom held out the sketchbook. Yes, that was him all right, sprawled on the bed, fast asleep, with his breeches unbuttoned and his cock peeping out.

Mortification heated his face, and then he looked again. Tom hadn't made him look comic or foolish—he'd made him look beautiful, like a fallen angel.

Lucas looked more closely. This wasn't one of Tom's two-minute sketches. This had taken time. Hours. The shading, the way light fell across the planes of his face . . . Jesus, he could practically see every hair on his head. "How long was I asleep?"

"Couple of hours."

Lucas flicked back a page and there was his cock—just his cock—rising from its nest of hair, thick and sturdy.

Lucas's thoughts lurched to a halt. His lips parted in horror. His gaze jerked to Tom.

Tom was eyeing him warily.

Lucas looked back down at the drawing and felt a surge of anger. A violation of privacy, that's what this sketch was.

"I wanted to draw you while I remembered how you looked," Tom said, in a neutral voice.

Lucas swallowed, and tried to tamp down his anger. "Why?"

"Because you're fucking magnificent."

His gaze jerked back to Tom's.

"You'd put Goliath to shame."

Lucas felt himself blush. He hastily closed the sketchbook.

"You've a cock like an ox's, Lu."

Lucas felt his blush spread, down his throat, to the tips of his ears, across his scalp. He thrust the sketchbook at Tom. "Well, yours looks like it's wearing a helmet."

Tom's brow creased. "What?"

"It looks like it's wearing a helmet," Lucas muttered. "You know, one of those Greek ones. Corinthian." *Take the damned sketchbook.*

Tom stopped looking wary. His eyes lit with laughter. "I'm going to call it that from now on: the Corinthian." He took the sketchbook and flipped to a new page. "And I'm calling yours the Ox."

Lucas reached for his tankard and took a hasty swallow. The ale was lukewarm and flat. He gulped another mouthful, and sat at the table. A pile of smaller sketchbooks caught his eye. He took one at random and hastily thumbed through it. Portugal.

He slowed, turning the pages, looking at the sketches of

soldiers. Was Tom's colonel one of these men? He flicked over a page—and halted. Good-looking, Tom had said. Clever. Brave. Liked to joke. "This is him, isn't it?" Jealousy roughened his voice. "Your colonel."

"Armagh sold out before Portugal." Tom plucked the sketchbook from Lucas's hand, glanced at the page, and gave it back. "That's Major Reid. He was a damned good soldier, too. One of the best."

"Was?" Lucas looked at the strong, handsome, laughing face captured in a few slashing pencil strokes. "He died?"

"He sold out after Vimeiro," Tom said, and his tone held an odd note.

Lucas glanced at him. "What happened?"

Tom hesitated, and then shrugged. "Reid was an exploring officer. Reconnaissance. He used to go behind enemy lines in uniform."

"In *uniform*? But . . . wasn't that dangerous?"

Tom laughed. "Extremely dangerous." And then he grimaced.

"What?"

"They caught him. The French. Just before Vimeiro."

Lucas looked down at the handsome, laughing face Tom had sketched.

"We got him back the next day, but . . . they'd been a bit rough with him."

"That's why he sold out?"

"He sold out because he got the fever and it nearly killed him. Damned shame." Tom sighed, and looked at the litter of sketchbooks on the table. "I'm starving. Want to go downstairs and eat?"

THAT EVENING, WHEN Lucas retired to his bedchamber, he didn't suggest Tom remain in the taproom; instead, he diffidently said: "I'm going upstairs if . . . if you want to come?"

They went up the stairs together, and undressed together, and climbed into Lucas's bed together, and then the afternoon replayed itself: the bruising kisses, their cocks dueling in Tom's hand, the dizzying orgasm.

Lucas woke in the dark, cold hours of early morning. He lay on his side and Tom was curled around him, holding him, and he had the same feeling of being safe and warm and protected that he'd sometimes had when he was a child.

He quietly cataloged the sensations: Tom's breath feathering across the nape of his neck. Tom's warm, solid chest pressed to his back. Tom's arm heavy and possessive around his waist. Tom's legs half-entwined with his.

The sense of warmth and safety deepened. Contentment stirred in Lucas's blood and he knew—just as he'd known that afternoon—that he'd never been as happy as he was right now, in this cozy nest of a bed.

He laid his hand over Tom's and interlaced their fingers and slid back into sleep. When he next woke it was daylight and Tom was gone. Only a dent in the pillow showed where he'd been.

Chapter Nine

October 10th, 1808
Whiteoaks, Wiltshire

TOM HADN'T VISITED Whiteoaks in more than two years. It hadn't changed: a glittering, sharp-edged marble palace surrounded by perfectly sculpted parkland.

The curricle's arrival brought Kemps hurrying down the long sweep of marble stairs.

Lucas's oldest brother Robert—who'd inherited the palace a decade ago—wrung his hand enthusiastically and Robert's wife, Almeria, embraced him and kissed him on each cheek, and their children pressed forward, half-shy, half-eager, calling him Uncle Tom.

It felt almost like coming home. He'd spent months of his life at Whiteoaks—practically every holiday while he was at school and university, almost every furlough since joining the army. He climbed the familiar stairs and entered the familiar bedchamber, the bedchamber he'd always had, across from

Lucas's, with a view over the park. When he stepped into the room he had the oddest sensation that the clock had turned back and he was eight years old again, accompanying Lucas home from Eton for the first time.

Tom stripped off his gloves and turned on his heel, and drank in the quiet grandeur of the room—the silk-covered walls, the four-poster bed with its blue and silver hangings, the Aubusson carpet, the moonlit landscape by Joseph Wright above the fireplace—and then he mentally placed it alongside the memory of his room at Riddleston Hall, small and dark and shabby, and gave a soft laugh. *And Lucas wondered why I never invited him home.*

But it hadn't been just the shabbiness; it had been his father, too—the flaring rages, the drunkenness.

Tom grimaced, and turned to the footman who'd been detailed to wait on him. "I'd like a bath, please, Joseph."

After the bath, Tom visited his favorite room at Whiteoaks: the gallery. He had to traverse almost a quarter of a mile of corridors to get there, but every staircase and every corner held memories. Here was the alcove where he and Lucas had hidden to ambush Julia and her cousin, Tish; and there the window seat from where Tish and Julia had ambushed them in return; this was the staircase whose banister they'd all slid down, shrieking; and that the door they'd tried to balance a bucket of water on top of—and failed; and over there was the window from which all four of them had watched Robert propose to Almeria in the garden. That last memory was the oldest of the lot, nineteen years ago now.

By the time he reached the long gallery, Tom's mood was verging on melancholy. So many memories—and all of them with Julia in them. He almost expected to hear her voice echoing gaily in the corridors, almost expected to hear her rapid footsteps, her irrepressible laugh. A door opened ahead and a woman emerged, and for a brief, disorienting moment he saw her as Julia—and then he blinked and realized it was a housemaid.

The housemaid gave him a startled look and a curtsy.

Tom dipped his head in return, and stepped into the gallery, and paused. Paintings. Hundreds of paintings.

He exhaled slowly, and began an unhurried circuit, the landscapes first, and then, when he couldn't avoid it any longer, the portraits.

The Kemps had a strong family likeness: large-boned, fair-haired, handsome. Here was the nabob who'd amassed such an extraordinary fortune in India, here was the son who'd married into the gentry and produced eight children, and here were the eight children, from Robert down to Lucas and Julia.

Julia looked like a changeling, a dark-haired little pixie in a family of blond giants.

Tom halted in front of the painting of Lucas and Julia. As portraits went, it was a fairly good one. Julia was prettier than she'd been in reality, but portraitists tended to do that: make eyes more lustrous, hair glossier, teeth pearlier. A subtle flattery that injured no one.

There'd been no need to enhance Lucas's appearance; he already looked like a Greek god made flesh.

Other than Julia's prettiness there were no flaws to the portrait—except that it was *flat*. There was no sense at all of who Lucas and Julia were. The artist had failed to capture Lucas's quiet reserve and Julia's vivacity. They might as well have been wax effigies, not people.

Tom stepped closer and examined the two faces. Lucas and Julia hadn't looked like siblings, let alone twins—except when they smiled, and then the similarity leapt to one's eye. But if the artist had seen that fleeting likeness, he'd been unable to render it on the canvas. All the portrait showed was how *un*alike Lucas and Julia had been. Lucas tall, Julia short. Lucas brawny, Julia slight. Lucas golden-haired and blue-eyed, Julia dark.

Their differences had gone deeper than mere appearance; they'd been opposites, two halves of a whole—Julia, exuberant and full of mischief, her tongue running on wheels, enjoying being the center of attention, delighting in making people laugh; Lucas quiet and steady and watchful. Julia messy, shedding hair-pins and tearing flounces; Lucas immaculate. Julia always plunging into trouble; Lucas rescuing her. It was Julia who'd fallen into the lake; Lucas who'd pulled her out. Julia who'd climbed a tree Lucas had deemed unsafe; Lucas who carried her home when she'd tumbled from it. It wasn't that Lucas lacked courage—he'd climbed a much higher tree—but he considered his risks before he took them, whereas Julia, spontaneous and reckless, had never considered risks at all.

And she had died because of that recklessness—putting an unfamiliar horse at a fence it couldn't jump, something Lucas would never do. Lucas had never overfaced a horse in his life; he had too much good sense, too much innate caution.

Tom stared soberly at the portrait. Twins, and yet so different. Gravity and Levity, someone had dubbed them once, but as sobriquets went, it had missed its mark. Lucas liked to laugh, he just did it more quietly than Julia. He'd done *everything* more quietly than Julia.

Tom studied the painting. *This isn't how I would have painted them.* In his portrait Julia would have been at the center, talking animatedly, not pretty, but lively, her hands outflung expressively, and Lucas would have been off to one side, leaning against the wall, smiling as he watched, his pride in her clear to read on his face.

Two halves of a whole—and now Julia was dead.

Chapter Ten

LUCAS ATE HIS dinner without tasting it. The feeling that he was missing a limb, that part of him had been amputated, was back.

For the past sixteen months he'd carried that feeling with him—and for four days it had gone. Four days when his every thought and emotion had revolved around Tom: panic and shame, passion and guilt, and happiness. All wiped away, now that he was back at Whiteoaks.

He ate mechanically, smiled mechanically, spoke mechanically, aware of Robert watching him out of the corner of his eye and Almeria sending him worried glances.

Tom was worried, too. Lucas could see it on his face. There was no merriment in those green eyes tonight.

Lucas chewed and swallowed, chewed and swallowed, and finally dinner was over. Almeria and the girls withdrew. The brandy and port were placed on the table.

"When's everyone else arriving?" Tom asked.

Lucas listened with half an ear, sipping his brandy, wishing he could drink the whole bottle and then climb the stairs to his bed and pull the covers over his head and sleep forever. A name caught his attention. "Tish? When does she get here?"

"Next month," Robert said.

Lucas nodded, and looked at the brandy decanter, and resolutely didn't pour himself another glass.

"Shall we join the ladies?" Robert said.

They filed out of the dining room. Tom caught Lucas's wrist, halting him. "Lu, are you all right?"

No. He felt numb, frozen, as if everything inside him had congealed. "Perfectly," he said.

"No, you're not."

"Tired," Lucas said.

"It's more than that." Tom touched the back of Lucas's hand, a light, fleeting caress.

A surge of panic broke through the numbness. Lucas recoiled, his heart hammering. "Not here. Someone will see." And he turned and almost ran to the drawing room.

TOM TRIED TO speak with him again before bed, halting him in the corridor outside their rooms. "Lu—"

"Not here! Someone might see!"

"There's no one here. Look, empty." Tom gestured along the corridor in both directions.

"Someone might come," Lucas said stubbornly.

Tom ignored this comment. His expression was uncharacteristically grim. "Something's wrong. Is it Julia?"

Lucas turned his head away. *Of course it's Julia.*

Tom took his hand. "Lu . . ."

"Not here!" Lucas tore his hand free and shoved Tom away so hard that he almost fell over. He wrenched open the door to his room and fled inside, slamming it shut behind him. His breath was rapid and shallow, panicked.

"Sir?" Smollet said, lifting his eyebrows.

Lucas caught his breath. He essayed a stiff smile and an attempt at cheerfulness. "Lord, I'm tired."

LUCAS'S SECOND-OLDEST BROTHER, Hugh, arrived the next morning with his wife. His youngest sister, Sophia, and her husband and children and two nursemaids arrived later that afternoon. Tom tried three times to speak privately with him, but each time Lucas pushed him away. *I shouldn't have brought him here. He'll betray us.*

The next morning, he hid in the library with a book, but Tom found him there. "Look, Lu—"

"No!" Lucas said, pushing past him, heading for the door.

Tom caught his wrist in a grip like an iron manacle. "For God's sake, stop running away!"

Lucas tried to jerk free.

Tom tightened his grip, digging his fingers in painfully.

"Let go of me!" Lucas hissed. His numb grief was gone; in its place was panic. "Hugh's a *clergyman.*"

"So?"

"So, if he sees us—"

"If he sees us he won't think twice about it. He's seen us together thousands of times." Impatience was tight on Tom's face, making him look sterner, older. "We're going riding this afternoon. Just you and I. Two o'clock."

Lucas shook his head.

"For Christ's sake, Lu, if we don't spend time together people will think something's wrong." Tom released his wrist, and poked him in the sternum with hard fingers, pushing Lucas back a step. "Riding. At two."

LUCAS RELUCTANTLY WENT RIDING at two o'clock. The horse caught his tension once he'd mounted, prancing and sidling in the stableyard, but Tom made no attempt to talk, setting the pace first at a brisk trot, and then a canter. By the time they reached the Marlborough Downs, Lucas felt the tension in his muscles starting to unravel.

The downs were good galloping country. They rode hard, not talking, and when they finally pulled up, Lucas felt more himself than he had in months.

Tom came up alongside him—not too close, not too far— and Lucas was abruptly ashamed of the way he'd behaved the past two days. Whatever else Tom was to him, he was his best friend.

"Thanks," he said gruffly. "I needed that."

Tom nodded.

They rode back more slowly, dropped down off the downs into the Whiteoaks park, trotted through the winter-bare blue-bell dell, jumped the stream. "I want to take a look at the folly," Tom said. "Do you mind?"

Lucas shook his head.

Whiteoaks' folly sat atop an outcrop of rock amid several acres of woodland, a little ruined castle with a dungeon and a tumbledown tower and a secret passage. They left the horses at the bottom and climbed the steps to the grassy courtyard.

Lucas felt his mood darken. They'd spent hours playing here as children, he and Tom, Julia and Tish. Hide-and-seek, ambushes, battles, play-acting. The great stone walls still seemed to echo with their voices. If he listened hard enough, maybe he'd hear Julia.

"The dungeon still got those ridiculous chains?" Tom asked.

Lucas nodded.

They clattered down the stairs to the dungeon, where daylight shone in through an iron grille, illuminating heavy chains dangling on one wall. Tom uttered a half-laugh and shook his head. "So *faux*." And then he turned to Lucas and the amusement drained from his face and something fierce and intent took its place. "Right."

Lucas took a wary step backwards. "Right, what?"

"This," Tom said, and then it was the Brook Street Mews all over again: Tom shoving him back against the wall, kissing him until Lucas could no longer think, then kneeling and sucking him to an orgasm so intense he saw stars.

Lucas leaned against the wall afterwards, trembling, dazed. Dimly, he was aware of Tom still at his feet, refastening his breeches. His thoughts lurched and staggered in his head as if he was drunk. *Jesus.* He slid bonelessly down the wall until he sat alongside Tom.

Tom put an arm around him and pulled him close.

Lucas rested his head on Tom's shoulder. He felt like an egg that someone had broken. He was in a million pieces. A million tiny pieces. He drew in a shaking breath. It hitched in his throat, caught in his chest—and then, to his horror, he started to cry.

Tom tightened his grip. "It's all right, Lu. It's all right."

Lucas cried harder than he'd ever cried in his life, so hard he could barely breathe, and Tom held him, and rocked him, and whispered, *It's all right, Lu. It's all right.*

Finally, the tears stopped, but he didn't pull away, and Tom didn't stop holding him. His breathing steadied, the tears dried on his cheeks, and still they sat, huddled against the wall in the dungeon. "I felt her die," Lucas whispered. "I was on my way back from Marlborough, and I felt it. I *knew*. I knew she was dead."

Tom's arms tightened around him. He pressed a kiss into Lucas's hair. "I know I'm not Julia, but I will always be here for you. *Always*."

"I know," Lucas whispered. "I know."

WHITEOAKS BECAME EASIER to bear after that. They went for daily rides, and somehow those rides always ended up at the folly, and they'd go down into the dungeon or climb the ruined tower, and Tom would ask if he could kiss him, and Lucas always said yes, because when Tom kissed him, the world fell away and he felt happy. And after the kisses Tom would whisper in his ear *Do you want my mouth or my hand?* and he always said the same thing: *Your hand*, because when Tom used his hand it felt like they were making love—Tom pressing him against the wall, the two of them straining together, their cocks striving in Tom's hand. Afterwards, when they stood leaning into each other, panting, the urge to cry would come again, but he always managed to hold it back.

During those moments in the folly the aching sense of loss, of amputation, went away, and even though it returned afterwards, it was never as bad as it had been. Lucas found it easier to smile and pretend that all was well. Robert stopped watching him so worriedly and Almeria no longer glanced at him every ten minutes. Robert's sons came home from Eton for a few days and spent most of their time sliding down the banisters. Tom joined in. "Come on, Lu!" he cried, as he swooped past. So Lucas did. By the time he reached the bottom, he was laughing.

It was the first time he'd laughed in sixteen months. It felt good.

More of his relatives arrived—brothers, sisters, cousins, nephews, nieces—gathering for the annual Kemp house party. Whiteoaks became busier, noisier. October became November. Tom's general wrote to say that the inquiry was finally starting, but it would be some weeks before his testimony was required.

"Guess who's arriving today," Tom said one afternoon, when they stood in the ruined tower looking down at the grassy courtyard.

Lucas leaned against the stone wall, feeling sated and relaxed. "Tish?"

"No, worse luck. Bernard."

Lucas groaned. Bernard Trentham. His second least favorite cousin. "Please tell me Caroline's not coming."

"She's not."

"Thank God for small mercies." If Bernard was his second least favorite cousin, Bernard's sister Caroline was his least favorite.

"Tish gets here next week."

"Good." He felt a pang of grief, because Tish and Julia had been best friends, and thinking of Tish always made him think of Julia. *But at least I have Tom,* and he shifted his weight so that his shoulder pressed against Tom's, and took comfort in his nearness, his warmth.

"Lu . . . you remember George Trentham?"

"Uncle George? My mother's brother? Of course I remember him."

"He never married."

"No."

"And he wasn't in the petticoat line, was he?"

Lucas shrugged. "Not that I ever heard."

"I remember he had a great friend, always traveled with him."

"John Wallace? Lord, yes, they were as close as brothers. Did everything together. Even shared the same townhouse in London. Never saw one without the other."

"Lu . . . do you think they were lovers?"

"Uncle George?" Lucas recoiled. "Of course not!"

Tom laughed, and shook his head. "If you could see your face, Lu." He leaned close and kissed Lucas's cheek. "You are so straitlaced."

Lucas flushed. "Uncle George was not a gentleman of the back door," he said stiffly.

Tom looked amused. "How do you know?"

"He was a respectable man. They both were! Everyone liked them!"

"So?"

Lucas turned his head away. He frowned down at the little courtyard below, with its grass and its tumbled blocks of stone and the crumbling wall on the far side with its huge gothic arch. For a moment, he saw Uncle George in his mind's eye— the round apple-red cheeks, the bristling white eyebrows, the twinkling eyes—and heard his deep, rich chuckle. Uncle George had been a *good* man, generous and kind and jovial.

Which doesn't mean that he wasn't a back door usher, a little voice pointed out at the back of his head.

Lucas rejected this thought, but it kept nibbling away inside his skull until he had to look at it squarely. Had Uncle George and John Wallace been lovers?

The more he thought about it, the more he thought that Tom was right. Uncle George had been a bachelor his whole life. So had John Wallace. They'd done everything together, even shared a house together.

"They might have been," Lucas said finally, grudgingly, and he glanced at Tom and found he was looking at him. "Maybe," he said, and then after a moment, even more grudgingly, "Probably."

Tom smiled a faint, unreadable smile, but said nothing.

They stood there in silence, and then Tom laughed, and said, "If Bernard knew——"

"He'd have an apoplexy."

Mischief lit Tom's face. "What a marvelous thought. I must tell him."

"Don't you dare!" Lucas said—and realized Tom was teasing him. "You're a damned loose screw," he said severely.

Tom grinned. "And you're a nodcock." He leaned in and kissed Lucas lightly—and Lucas kissed him back—and then the afternoon dissolved into bone-melting pleasure again, and he was happy, purely happy.

And after that, they rode back to Whiteoaks and discovered that Bernard Trentham had arrived.

Chapter Eleven

BERNARD TRENTHAM WAS ONLY HALF a dozen years older than
Tom, but he behaved as if he was in his fifties: staid, pompous,
disapproving. But Bernard had been a fifty-year-old his whole
life—or at least as long as Tom had known him, which was
almost twenty years.

Bernard shook Tom's hand and made the same not-quite-
joke he always did: "Ah, the Honorable Thomas."

Tom smiled tightly.

"And how is your brother, the earl?" Bernard asked.

"I haven't seen him yet." And he realized, with a faint
sense of shock, that he hadn't written to tell Daniel he was
back in England, hadn't even thought about Daniel. He felt a
twinge of guilt. *I must visit him before I leave England.*

Bernard droned on and it was nearly ten minutes before
Tom escaped. "Christ," he said to Lucas, in the privacy of the
library. "He gets worse every time I see him. Poor Tish, having
him as a stepbrother."

Lucas put down his book. "Did he mention his mother, Lady Mary?"

"Yes."

"And his grandfather, the duke?"

"Yes."

"And his father-in-law, the viscount?"

"Yes." Tom crossed to the fire and leaned against the mantelpiece. "Thank God he hasn't brought that prim, fubsy-faced wife of his."

"You mean, the viscount's daughter?"

Tom gave him a look.

Lucas grinned—and he looked so beautiful, so golden, that Tom's heart tightened painfully in his chest.

He looked away, swallowed, looked back. "Two of Tish's suitors are coming. Bernard invited them."

Lucas lost his grin. He blinked. "What? *Bernard* invited them to Whiteoaks?"

"Robert invited them, at Bernard's request."

Lucas frowned. "Robert did? Dash it, he knows she gets hounded enough in London—"

"Don't blame Robert. I think Bernard badgered him until he gave in."

Lucas grunted. The beautiful, golden grin was gone.

"One of them's that idiot Stapleton, but the other one's Henry Wright. You remember Henry? A year ahead of us at school?"

Lucas nodded.

"Bernard called him Sir Henry."

"His father died a couple of months ago. Left him in a devil of a mess. Debts up to his eyebrows."

Tom grimaced. "Shame. I always liked Henry. Very up-front."

"And in need of an heiress now."

"At least he won't hound Tish. He'll ask, she'll say no, that'll be it." He shrugged. "I understand why Henry's after her, but why is Stapleton? I thought he inherited a fortune."

"Run through it already. Gambler."

Tom thought of his father. He kicked the grate with his boot. Gamblers and fortunes were a bad combination. "What's Tish's count this year, d' you know?"

"Proposals? Fifteen, last I asked."

"A coachwheel says she's past twenty by now."

Lucas considered this for a moment, and then nodded. "You're on."

Tom pushed away from the mantelpiece. "Dinner in half an hour." He crossed to the armchair and ran his fingers through Lucas's hair—a light, swift caress that was over before Lucas could stiffen in alarm—and then continued to the door. "Come on, you know you take forever to change."

AFTER DINNER, ONCE the ladies had withdrawn and the decanters of port and brandy had been placed on the table, talk turned to boxing. The upshot of that conversation was an informal sparring session the next day, in one of the unused salons. Eight men gathered: the four Kemp brothers, three Kemp cousins, and one brave brother-in-law. Tailcoats were shucked and footwear removed.

Tom, who was a mediocre boxer, fished his sketchbook out of his breast pocket and opened it to a fresh page.

The Kemps were a family of large, strong, athletic men, and Lucas was one of the largest and strongest, but for all his brawniness he was light on his feet, fast and agile. God, he was magnificent—and yet completely unaware of his magnificence, just as he was unaware of the admiration he was garnering as he demonstrated a number of moves with his cousin, Arnold—the common parry and opposite parry, the side step and drop step, the chancery hold and pinion. When he laid Arnold on the floor with a cross-buttock throw that even Tom could see had been superb, Lucas didn't swagger, because Lucas didn't know *how* to swagger; he just held out his hand to Arnold and hauled him to his feet again.

The men broke into pairs to practice the moves; the room filled with the sound of panted breaths and scuffing feet, grunts and laughter. Tom made quick sketches—knuckles and knotted brows, grins and grimaces. Half an hour passed. Waistcoats and neckcloths were flung aside and shirt-sleeves rolled up. The room began to smell strongly of sweat. Tom's sketchbook was nearly full. He closed it and watched Lucas spar with his second-oldest brother, the Very Reverend Hugh Kemp.

No one looking at Lucas would believe that he'd been a virgin until last month. He was so damned masculine, so virile, the absolute epitome of manliness.

"No," Lucas said, when Hugh attempted a chancery hold, "Like this," and Hugh, who was pompous and starchy and destined to be an archbishop if ever Tom had seen a man destined to be an archbishop, didn't bristle, but instead paid frowning attention to Lucas's instruction.

The pugilists broke for ale. Lucas came to stand with him. "Sure you don't want to spar?" he asked, gulping down his ale. "Good exercise."

"I'd rather sketch." Boxing wasn't his sport. Swords were another matter; he could hold his own against Lucas when it came to fencing. But if he ever crossed foils with Lucas, he wanted the two of them to be alone, so that when they grew hot and sweaty and out of breath, they could—

Tom stopped that thought in its tracks. *Down, boy,* he told his cock, before it could get any ideas. He took a hasty sip of ale, and another, and found himself gazing at Lucas's open shirt collar. He imagined kissing Lucas there, imagined tasting his warm, salty skin, and stifled a sigh of longing. "Riding, later?"

Lucas's cheeks became faintly pink. He nodded.

After the ale had been drunk, Robert asked the two most skillful boxers—Lucas and his next-oldest brother, Edward— for an exhibition bout.

Tom watched the two men take their places. Edward belonged to the sporting set in London. He was a regular out and outer, a top o' the trees—and he had the swagger to go with it. The swagger Lucas lacked.

A stranger might mistake Lucas's quiet self-assurance for shyness, but Lucas wasn't shy. He was as confident as Edward, just without his braggadocio.

But he's not confident about sex, Tom thought. *He's shy in the bedroom.* And he remembered Lucas's blushes, his tentative explorations, and felt a pang of emotion: tenderness and protectiveness mixed together.

"Ready?" Robert said.

Talk ceased. All eyes turned to the two brothers: Lucas standing calmly, Edward strutting. Tom didn't begrudge Edward his posturing and his bravado. Everyone—including Edward—knew that Lucas was going to win this fight.

"No blows to the face," Edward said. "I like my nose the way it is, little brother."

Tom had watched Lucas box hundreds of times—at Eton, at Oxford, at Jackson's Saloon in London—and whenever he watched Lucas fight he always came to the same conclusions. It wasn't Lucas's size and strength and speed that made him so formidable an opponent. It wasn't that his science was excellent—although it *was* excellent. What made Lucas formidable was his calmness, his almost introspective focus. Lucas's temper never frayed when he was boxing, he never became frustrated or impatient or reckless—and that, to Tom's mind, was what gave Lucas his edge.

The bout was a friendly one—no blood, just sweat. Lots of sweat. After fifteen minutes, Edward was red-faced and laboring and beginning to flail wildly. "For God's sake," he rasped, breath whistling in his throat. "Finish me off!" And so Lucas did, with another one of his superb cross-buttock throws.

Edward made no attempt to climb to his feet. He lay where he'd fallen, theatrical in his defeat, gasping and groaning.

The man alongside Tom let out a sigh. "Damn, Lucas is good."

Tom glanced at him. It was Lucas's cousin, Arnold.

Arnold's expression mirrored the tone of his voice: admiration, underlain by a rueful envy. He wanted to be Lucas.

Tom thought about Lucas's years of lonely celibacy. *No, Arnold, you don't want to be Lucas.* And then he thought about riding out to the folly later that afternoon and how close he and Lucas would be—mouths kissing, cocks touching—and how *not* lonely Lucas would be then.

He looked across at Lucas, sweaty and magnificent in the middle of the salon, quietly laughing at his brother's histrionics, and all the air left his lungs, as if it was he who lay winded on the floor and not Edward.

I love you, Lu. I will always love you.

SIX DAYS LATER, he and Lucas were trotting slowly through the park, and Tom was happy and relaxed and his cock was still pleasantly warm, when they came into the avenue of oaks and saw a lone figure walking—the height, the thin, boyish figure, the austere elegance of the woman's clothes . . . there was no one it could be but Letitia Trentham.

"That's Tish!" Tom said, and he whooped loudly, startling his mount, and together he and Lucas thundered down the long avenue.

Tom whooped again as they swept past Tish in a swirl of dead leaves, and then he jumped down from the saddle and strode back to her and hugged her, lifting her off her feet. "Tish, m' love. God, but it's good to see you." And Lucas hugged her, too, and they were all laughing, and it was so *right*, the four of them being together again, and Tom looked around for Julia, *knowing* she was there—but she wasn't.

His laughter drained away, but the sense that Julia was standing beside him didn't vanish. It was so strong, so *real*, that he actually looked around a second time.

"When did you arrive?" Lucas asked.

Tom brought his attention back to Tish.

"An hour ago," she said.

It was nearly two years since he'd last seen Tish, but she hadn't changed at all. She had a face that begged to be drawn. Not because it was perfect in its symmetry, like Lucas's, but because it *wasn't*. All her features were slightly out of balance —nose too long, mouth too wide, cheekbones too prominent— until she smiled, when suddenly everything *was* in balance. She was smiling now, as she asked, "How are you both?"

"In fine form," Lucas said. "What's the count now?"

"Eighteen so far this year."

Darn it. Tom dug in his pocket and flipped a half-crown at Lucas.

Lucas caught it. "You'll find a couple of 'em here this week, Tish. Bernard nagged m' brother into inviting them.

Stapleton's already arrived, and Henry Wright's coming on Monday. Wright's a decent fellow—he was at Eton with us—but I don't think much of Stapleton."

Tom fished another half-crown from his pocket and waggled it between his fingers. "A new wager. Stapleton *and* Wright to propose by the end of the week."

Lucas pursed his lips, as if debating this offer.

"I *am* here," Tish said indignantly.

Tom grinned at her. "I know, love." And even if Julia was no longer with them it felt marvelous to be together again, teasing each other. He stuffed the coin back in his pocket. "Walk back with us?"

Tish tucked her hand into the crook of his arm. "I met an acquaintance of yours in London last week. Icarus Reid. He was a major before he sold out."

"Reid?" Tom said, startled.

"He said he'd be passing through Wiltshire. I told him you were here, suggested he look you up."

"I hope he does," Tom said. "Good man, Reid."

THAT EVENING, AFTER a rowdy game of Speculation, Tish said to him in an undervoice, "Come riding with me tomorrow morning. Before church. I need to talk with you."

Tom grinned at her. "An assignation, Tish?"

"Eight o'clock," Tish said, not grinning back.

Tom lifted his eyebrows. Was this something to do with Major Reid? He laid a hand to his breast and gave a bow. "I'll be there, dear heart." But Tish didn't smile, she merely said, "Thank you."

Tom watched her leave the room, tall and thin and elegant. *What's this about?*

Chapter Twelve

November 13th, 1808
Whiteoaks, Wiltshire

TISH MET HIM in the stableyard, austere and angular in a navy blue riding habit. They mounted, and trotted from the yard. Tom tried to tease her into smiling. "This may be the most exciting morning of my life. Trysting with an heiress! Is it to be a special license, Tish, or do you want the banns to be read?"

Tish's mouth tucked in at the corners. "Tom, do be serious."

Not until you smile properly. "But I feel it's only fair to tell you that my heart belongs to another!"

"I want to talk about Lucas."

The levity drained from him. "What about him?"

"How is he? Truly?"

Tom had a flash of memory: Lucas crying so hard it seemed that he would turn himself inside out.

He looked away, swallowed, found enough of his voice to say, "Let's canter."

By the time they were up on the downs, he had control of his vocal cords. He halted at a viewpoint and stared down at Whiteoaks. *How much should I tell her?*

He glanced at Tish, silent alongside him. "Have you seen much of Lucas this past year?"

Tish shook her head. "He's been dealing with his godfather's estate. He only came back to town last month. He seemed . . . I thought he seemed happier. He wasn't wearing blacks."

"When did you see him last?"

"The beginning of October. I asked him to dine with me on his birthday, but he'd already accepted an invitation elsewhere."

"Had he?" Tom grimaced, and looked away. "He didn't go. I arrived in London the evening of his birthday, went round to his rooms, found him sitting in the dark with the fire gone out, so drunk he couldn't even stand up." He paused—and then decided to tell her it all. "He'd been crying."

Tish stared at him, aghast. "But he seemed almost his old self!"

"He's not," Tom said flatly. "He puts on a good act, but he has days where I don't think he'd even get out of bed—let alone shave or dress—if not for that man of his."

Tish said nothing; she just stared at him, her mouth half-open, as if she wanted to speak but couldn't find any words.

"You know how wounded animals hide themselves away? That's what he did after Julia died—and I understand he needed to be alone afterwards—you don't have to tell me how close they were—but he needs to crawl out of his cave and learn how to be happy without her."

"I thought he had."

"No." Tom shook his head. "I asked for an extended leave of absence. Wellesley gave me until the end of the year."

"For Lucas?'

"Of course, for Lucas!"

"Can I help?"

"I don't know. I don't even know that *I* can help." He was giving Lucas everything he had, giving him his body, his heart, his soul—but he didn't know whether it was enough—or whether Lucas truly wanted it. "I don't know that coming here was a good idea. This place is full of Julia." He shook his head again. "Come on, let's ride."

WHEN THEY WERE BACK in the long avenue again, the bare oak branches meeting overhead in a complicated pattern, Tish asked, "How are you enjoying soldiering?"

Tom shrugged. "Oh, I like it well enough."

Tish looked at him with those astute eyes of hers. "You'd rather sell out and be an artist?"

He gave an uncomfortable laugh. "You know me too well."

"*Could* you sell out?"

"Only if I marry an heiress." Tom leered at her cheerfully. "What do you say, Tish? Want to marry a youngest son with not a penny to his name?"

"Your heart belongs to someone else," Tish reminded him.

He lost his smile. "So it does."

The horses' hooves clomped somberly on the dead leaves. Tish took a deep breath. "Tom? If you had twenty thousand pounds, would you sell out?"

"Yes." Hell, he'd sell out if he had *two* thousand pounds. "But I don't." He turned the subject "There's to be a ball this week. Did Almeria tell you?"

"Tom . . . I can *give* you twenty thousand pounds."

"What? Don't be ridiculous."

"I'm not being ridiculous. Let me give you twenty thousand. Then you can sell out!"

For half a second he let himself imagine it: He could stay in England. His life would be pencils and charcoal and paint, line and form, light and shade, color—and Lucas. Lucas morning, afternoon, and night. And then he said, firmly, "Thank you, but no."

"Why not?"

Because I have some pride. Tom reached over and caught her hand and kissed her gloved knuckles. "Tish, I love you dearly, but I *won't* take your money."

"But—"

"No." He released her hand. "Don't feel sorry for me, Tish. Soldiering suits me well enough. I'm better off than a lot of younger sons!" And then he thought of Daniel. "And heirs, for that matter. I'm a thousand times better off than m' brother, saddled with Father's debts. Or Henry Wright. Poor devils."

"Yes, but if I give you—"

"Lord, Tish, you're like a terrier at a rabbit hole! I *don't* want your money."

Tish gave an exasperated sigh.

They reached the end of the avenue. The gleaming marble frontage of Whiteoaks came into sight and Tom thought—not for the first time—that the nabob might have had a head for business, but he hadn't had an eye for architecture. Lord, what a monstrosity of a home he'd built, all sharp, unforgiving angles and perfect, unflinching symmetry, everything so white and glittering that it made one's eyes wince.

"Tom . . . will you tell me about the Battle of Vimeiro?"

"Vimeiro?" Tom turned his head and stared at her. "What do you want to know?"

"Everything."

Tom shrugged. "The battle was straightforward. We outnumbered the French. Not many casualties."

"Did you fight?"

"Me? I carried orders, mostly."

"Carried orders?"

"The general can't be in more than one place, so his aides-de-camp relay his orders. Vimeiro was pretty busy—we were down a couple of officers—one drunk, the other missing—I went back and forth a score of times. Quite wore out my horse!"

They dismounted in the stableyard—and on their heels came another horse, ridden by a liveried servant. The man didn't dismount, but leaned low and passed something to one of the grooms.

"Lieutenant Matlock, sir?" the groom said. "A message for you."

"For me?" Tom took the letter and broke open the seal. His eyes skipped down to the signature at the bottom. Reid.

Memory of Vimeiro came flooding back. The things he'd not told Tish: the dead scouts, Major Reid.

Tom shook his head, banishing the memory, and read the message swiftly. "Tell him yes," he told the mounted servant. "Two o'clock."

"Yes, what?" Tish asked.

"Major Reid's in Marlborough. He's coming to visit this afternoon." He shoved the letter into his pocket. "Hurry up, Tish. We'll be late for church!"

Chapter Thirteen

MAJOR REID ARRIVED astride a great Roman-nosed gray. Tom almost didn't recognize him. *That's Reid? That skeleton dressed in riding clothes?*

He swallowed his shock. "Major Reid!" he called out, and strode across the stableyard to greet him.

Reid dismounted. "Matlock. How do you do?"

"Lord, Major, you look like death warmed over! Fever take you again, sir?"

Reid shrugged. "You know how it is."

Tom nodded. He'd seen soldiers worn to the bone by fever before. "Let me introduce you to m' host, Major, and then we'll have a chat about old times." But ten minutes of watching Reid make small talk with Robert and Almeria in the green and gold salon filled him with the conviction that something more than mere illness was wrong with Reid. The painful gauntness, the weariness etched into the man's face—those were the result of the fever—but underlying those things was something else, something that was brittle and hollow and bleak and altogether unlike the Reid he'd known.

If Reid had changed, he knew why: Because of what had happened at Vimeiro.

He slid Reid from the salon and took him round to the shrubbery, where Lucas and Tish waited. "I don't need to introduce you to Miss Trentham, do I?"

"No."

The four of them strolled in the shrubbery and Reid seemed to relax, to become more the man Tom knew—good-humored, easy-going—but he couldn't shake the feeling that Reid was indelibly altered, that he'd been damaged in some deep and terrible way.

After the shrubbery, they went inside and ate cake and macaroons, and after that they all rode out, parting company with Reid at the gatehouse. "Come again," Tom said. "Tomorrow afternoon? We can ride up on the downs."

Reid hesitated, and then agreed.

Tom watched him ride away, a large man grown far too thin. *He needs help.*

"So that's the famous major," Lucas said. "Not what I expected."

"Not what I expected either," Tom admitted. "He's altered almost past recognition."

THAT EVENING, AFTER dinner, Tish asked to see Tom's sketches of Portugal. Tom went up to his room and sorted through his sketchbooks, and hesitated for a moment, uncertain whether to show her the one with the musket ball in it or not—and then he remembered Lucas's reaction to it and put it firmly to one side.

The three of them settled in the library and Tish went through the first sketchbook, turning the pages slowly, studying each drawing, asking questions.

Halfway through the second sketchbook, she stopped. "My goodness." Her tone was incredulous. "That's Mr. Reid!"

Lucas craned closer. "So it is. Lord, I'd scarcely recognize him."

"I nearly didn't this afternoon," Tom said. "Got a deuce of a shock. Looks ten years older. Thin as a damned skeleton."

Tish went carefully through the sketchbooks. When she'd finished, she said, "Your landscapes are beautiful, but the people . . ." She looked down at the open sketchbook on her lap, lightly touched the portrait there. "How on earth do you do it, Tom?"

"Good, isn't he?" Lucas said, and Tom felt himself blush.

Tish closed the sketchbook and gave it back. "Tom . . . when I first met him, Reid told me a little about Vimeiro. He said he and his scouts were captured, and the scouts were killed."

Tom blinked. "Reid told you that?"

Tish nodded. "Do you know anything about it? Do you know what happened?"

"Know?" Tom grimaced. "I was the one who found him."

"Found him?"

Tom looked away from her. He stacked the sketchbooks. What had happened to Reid was not something he particularly wished to discuss.

"Was it very bad?" Tish asked hesitantly.

"Bad? Not really. Not like battle." Tom put the sketchbooks aside, got up, stirred the fire with the poker, added another log.

Behind him, Tish and Lucas were silent.

Finally, reluctantly, unwillingly, Tom returned to his armchair. "What did Reid tell you?"

"That he was caught close to dusk, when he met up with his scouts, and that the scouts were summarily executed as spies, but he wasn't, because he was in uniform."

Tom grunted. "The liaison officer was killed, too, and he *was* in uniform."

"Liaison officer?"

"Portuguese lieutenant. Pereira. Acted as translator. Reid can't speak Portuguese, y' know."

Tish raised her eyebrows. "They executed him, too?"

"No." Tom shifted uncomfortably in his armchair, shifted again, blew out a breath. *Oh, for God's sake, just tell them.* "The battle was over by midday. Reid still hadn't returned, been missing all night, so Wellesley sent me to look for him. Took half a dozen men with me."

It hadn't taken long to find Reid. Tom remembered that moment: the futile rage when he saw the bodies—and the utter relief when he realized Reid was still alive.

"And you found him?" Lucas said.

"Found them all, in a gully. Reid's rendezvous point. The scouts had been shot. The liaison officer . . ." He kicked one heel against the armchair. "Don't know what killed him, but I can guess."

Thock, thock, thock went his heel against the chair. With effort, he stilled the movement.

"What?" Lucas asked.

"They drowned him."

Tish put up her eyebrows. "Drowned him?"

"There was a creek." He saw it in his mind's eye: a rocky, narrow gully, a sluggish little creek, the water so shallow it wouldn't have come over the top of his riding boots. *But deep enough to drown a man if he can't fight back.* He discovered he was kicking the armchair again—and stopped himself.

"And . . . ?" Lucas prompted.

Fuck, just tell them. "Reid and Pereira were on the ground, bound hand and foot. Pereira was dead, Reid was alive. Both soaked to the bone. It hadn't rained. They'd been in the creek for sure."

Tish looked slightly ill. "What did Reid say?"

"Nothing, far as I know." *Thock, thock, thock.* He forced himself to stop kicking the armchair. "He was out cold when I found him, not breathing that well. Portugal in August, it's hot, but he was shivering like it was the middle of winter. He came down with a fever and inflammation of the lungs, was out of his mind for weeks, nearly died three or four times."

Tish looked down at her lap and twisted a fold of silk between her fingers. "Had he been injured at all?"

"No."

"Do you think . . . the French were torturing him?"

"What? No. Of course not!"

"What, then?"

Tom grimaced, and looked at the fire. "I think they were having some sport and it went too far." His boot began to swing again: *thock, thock.*

"Nasty," Lucas said quietly.

Tom shrugged. "Battle's far nastier. Wait till you've seen a man get disemboweled. Or a horse——" He stopped kicking the chair and sat upright. "I beg your pardon, Tish. Not a topic for your ears."

Tish surveyed him soberly. "You don't draw those things."

"Who would want to?"

Behind him, the library door opened. "There you are, Letitia! I've been looking everywhere for you."

Tom's back was to the door, but he recognized the voice. He pulled a face.

"Oh, Lord," Lucas muttered under his breath.

"What are you doing in here?" Bernard asked, in his fussy, disapproving fifty-year-old's voice.

"Looking through some of Tom's sketches," Lucas said mildly.

Bernard sniffed. "I should have thought daylight was better for that. Lucas, Thomas, if I may please have a private word with my stepsister?"

Tom climbed to his feet. He gathered up the sketchbooks. Together, he and Lucas left the library. "I don't know how Tish bears him," he muttered, once they were in the corridor.

"Got no choice, has she?"

Tom grunted. He didn't feel like returning to the drawing room and the tea tray and polite conversation. "Want to play billiards?"

Lucas shrugged. "Why not?"

Tom turned towards the great double staircase. "I'll take these upstairs. Be down in two minutes."

"Tom . . ."

He halted, and turned back. "What?"

Lucas's expression was serious. No, more than serious; frowning.

"What?" Tom said again.

"I always thought you liked it—soldiering—but you don't, do you?"

Tom opened his mouth, and closed it again.

"Whenever anyone asks you about it, you make it sound interesting and . . . and *fun*. I've never heard you talk about it the way you did tonight."

Tom shrugged, and looked away. "I like parts of it." *And parts of it I hate.* "It suits me a lot better than the church would have." He found a laugh. "Can you imagine me preaching morality?"

Lucas didn't return the laugh. "Can you sell out?"

Tom looked at him. The nabob's grandson who'd come into a small fortune when his father died, and inherited even more on his twenty-first birthday, whose godfather had left him a whole estate down in Cornwall, who'd never in his life—not once—had to worry about how much things cost, never had to decide between new boots or a new tailcoat, never had to travel by mail coach because it was all he could afford, never had to count his coins before ordering a meal.

You have no idea, do you?

"No," he said shortly, turning away. "I can't sell out."

"Tom, wait."

He turned back, and found himself almost hating Lucas for his wealth. "And before you offer it, I don't want your damned charity."

Lucas's face tightened, as if the words had been a slap.

Tom sighed. He didn't want to be having this conversation. Not now. Not ever. "I'm sorry. Let's not talk about this, Lu. All right?"

Lucas looked at him for a moment, and then nodded. A stiff little nod.

I've offended him. "I'm sorry," Tom said again.

Lucas stopped looking so stiff. This time he shook his head. He gave a wry smile, a wry shrug.

Tom's guilt intensified. Lucas had come into the world not only shod and hosed, but clutching a golden rattle. He should be arrogant and conceited. The miracle was that he wasn't. He never flaunted his money, never puffed himself off. He was quiet and steady and dependable and unpretentious.

And he's trying to help me.

"I'm sorry, Lu," he said quietly, and held out his hand. "I didn't mean to fly up into the boughs."

Lucas hesitated, and then reached out and touched his fingertips lightly, briefly.

Tom's chest tightened. He wanted to step close to Lucas and put his arms around him, right there in the corridor with a chandelier blazing overhead, where anyone could see them. *I love you.* He swallowed, and tried to find a smile. "I'll just take these sketchbooks upstairs. Be down in a couple of minutes."

Come upstairs with me, please. Hold me, please.

He bit the words back and turned away and climbed the stairs slowly, alone.

Chapter Fourteen

November 14th, 1808
Whiteoaks, Wiltshire

WHILE IT WAS enjoyable to go riding with Tish and Major Reid in the afternoon, it meant that Tom had to forgo his tryst with Lucas in the folly for the second day running. Tom wondered if Lucas missed it as much as he did—the physical closeness, breathing each other's breaths, their cocks sliding together in his hand, the sense that they were so close they were almost inside each other's skin.

Lucas didn't appear to miss it. He sat in the green and gold salon, eating plum cake and discussing his nephew's upcoming birthday, as if he weren't aching with need.

"He's mad about the knights of the Round Table," Lucas said. "Imagines himself as Sir Gawain."

Sir Gawain had been one of the chaste knights, as Tom recalled it—which brought to mind a joke that he couldn't relate right now, not with Tish sitting there, and Robert's eldest daughter, Selina. And then he recalled Lucas, tense with shame, almost crying when he admitted he couldn't have sex with women. Tom winced inwardly. *Don't* ever *make jokes about chastity in Lucas's hearing.*

He brought his attention back to the conversation, and discovered that Lucas was speaking to him.

"I was thinking . . . could you paint Sir Gawain, Tom?"

Tom shrugged, and reached for a macaroon. "Of course."

"If I model for Gawain, can you make me look like Oscar?"

"Of course." The boy was back at Eton now, but Tom had a couple of two-minute sketches of him.

He'd need a larger sheet of watercolor paper than he had, and an easel, but the Whiteoaks art room would have those. And he knew exactly the backdrop he wanted: the ruined castle. Tom opened his mouth to suggest this, but Tish beat him to it.

"What an excellent idea! And I know the perfect setting: the folly! We should all ride over there tomorrow afternoon."

Tom closed his mouth. *Actually, I was thinking just Lu and me.* And then he gave an internal shrug. They'd get bored soon enough, watching him sketch.

───────────

BUT HE DIDN'T START Sir Gawain the following day, because the sketching party became a picnic—not only Tish and Major Reid, but Sir Henry Wright, two of Lucas's nieces, and two servants.

Fuck, Tom thought, when he saw all the people assembled in the stableyard, and then he blew out a breath and told himself that he *liked* Tish's company, and Reid's, and Henry Wright's, and if he didn't get to touch Lucas until tomorrow, it wasn't the end of the world, even if it felt as if it was.

They all climbed the steps to the castle and entered the grassy courtyard. Sir Henry looked around and laughed and said, "Fabulous!"

Tom's grumpiness began to fade.

"Isn't it just? There's a dungeon *and* a secret passage," Tish said, and Sir Henry laughed again, and Tom found himself almost smiling.

When Sir Henry saw the rusted chains hanging on the dungeon wall, he laughed a third time and said, "This is almost too good to be true!"

Tom's smile became a grin. "Wait till you see the secret passage."

"Where is it?" Sir Henry demanded.

"You find it."

And after that, he enjoyed the afternoon, even though he didn't get to touch Lucas. *Tomorrow,* he told himself as he lounged in the grassy courtyard eating macaroons and listening to Lucas's nieces discuss the upcoming ball. *Tomorrow,* as he sipped lemonade and answered Sir Henry's questions about the army and what it was like to be a general's aide-de-camp. *Tomorrow,* as they all rode back through the park together.

They dismounted in the stableyard, and it was all laughter and bustle—grooms and horses and people milling around. Tom caught Lucas's elbow. "Tomorrow morning, straight after breakfast," he said, brusque and businesslike, as if it wasn't an assignation between lovers. "We'll make a start on that painting."

And tomorrow *did* come, and it was everything he'd hoped for—just he and Lucas alone in the folly, and when they made love in the dungeon, Lucas was as frantic as he was, and it was fast and fierce and almost desperate—and then they did it a second time, their kisses more leisurely, his hand slowly stroking them towards climax—and at the very end, Lucas cried out and Tom captured the sound with his mouth, just as he captured their seed in his handkerchief—and they stayed leaning into one another for several minutes, their cocks soft in his hand—and then Tom folded up the handkerchief and they buttoned their buttons and it was time to sketch.

HE DREW THE great gothic arch first and then positioned Lucas in a heroic pose: feet apart, legs braced, shoulders back. "Here, hold this," he said, giving Lucas a paintbrush. "Pretend it's a sword—a little lower—yes, perfect."

He stepped back. Fuck, Lucas was magnificent. Even holding that ridiculous paintbrush, he looked valiant and resolute and dauntless and quite stunningly masculine. "You should see yourself, Lu. You look like you've just stepped out of a Greek epic."

Lucas went faintly pink—and that was one of the nicest things about Lucas: for all his physical beauty, he hadn't an ounce of vanity. He checked his neckcloths in the mirror, but never his face.

Tom drew quickly, humming under his breath, sketching in the lines of Lucas's body: the strong throat, the broad shoulders, the muscular thighs.

Once the outlines were done, they packed up and rode back to Whiteoaks, and after lunch he got out his color box. He opened the lid. Lucas peered over his shoulder. "Those all the colors you've got? Twelve?"

"I can mix any color I want with these."

Lucas wasn't convinced. He dragged Tom off to the art room and showed him all the watercolor cakes.

Tom laughed. "Christ, Lu, there must be almost a hundred."

It was a visual feast: every color in Ackermann's catalog—Dragon's Blood, Chinese Vermilion, Iris Green—but although they looked beautiful laid out in their drawers, he knew most of the colors would swiftly fade. This bouquet of blues and yellows and reds and greens was for dabblers, for people who didn't understand paint; his tray of twelve colors was all he needed.

Tom laid down a graded wash of Prussian Blue for the sky, and left it to dry. The rest of the day sped past—riding with Tish and Reid and Sir Henry, the formal dinner, and after that, the ball, where he drank a little too much, and danced almost every dance, and flirted with all the pretty girls. The ballroom was crowded, and yet it seemed as if an invisible thread connected him to Lucas; he always knew where Lucas was, never had to crane his neck and search for him. They orbited each other on the dance floor, and the fleeting moments when their eyes met felt as intimate as kisses.

ON WEDNESDAY, TOM painted in the great gothic arch, the tumbled blocks of stone, the grass, the shadows. Lucas lounged against a crumbling wall and watched. Tom whistled under his breath, laying in each color, enjoying the simplicity of it—paint, water, brush—and yet also the challenge—the way the watercolors had a life of their own, a fluidity that was unpredictable. And underneath his pleasure in painting was pleasure in Lucas's quiet companionship, a deep contentment that hummed in his blood.

"You love it, don't you? Drawing. Painting."

He glanced at Lucas. "Yes."

He was painting in the last strokes of green when Tish burst into the courtyard, soaking wet.

Tom lowered his brush. "Tish?"

"Reid's horse refused at the stream," Tish said, and her voice was too high, too tight.

"Is he all right?" Lucas said sharply.

"Perfectly," Tish said. "Just wet. Can he borrow one of your horses, please?"

"Of course," Tom said, at the same time that Lucas said, "Take mine."

"He'll need a change of clothes," Tish said. She wasn't wearing gloves and her hands were wringing each other, white-knuckled. "Tom? Could he borrow some of yours?"

"Of course," he said again.

Lucas took the paintbrush. "Go back with them. I'll pack up here for you."

Tom looked at Tish's pale, taut face, and then glanced at Lucas. Julia had died after being thrown from her horse. *Will you be all right alone?*

Lucas seemed to understand the silent question, for he gave a short nod. "Go."

So Tom went, clattering down the stone steps to where the horses were tethered. And when he saw Major Reid, he understood Tish's agitation. The man was gray beneath his tan, shaking convulsively, his eyes almost wild.

Tom had a vivid flash of memory: a scrubby gully, a creek, Reid bound hand and foot, sodden, half-dead, his breath rattling in his chest.

Oh, fuck.

"Took a toss, did you?" he said cheerfully. "Lord, but you're wet, the pair of you!" And why was Tish wet, if it was

Reid who'd fallen? "You'll borrow my clothes, of course, Major! We're almost of a height."

Back at the stableyard, Tish took Tom's elbow in a pinching grip. "He needs something hot to drink," she hissed in his ear. "And some brandy."

"He'll get it," Tom said, detaching her hand and giving her cold fingers a squeeze. "Don't worry. You go and change."

He maintained a flow of light, cheerful conversation while he escorted Reid up to his room, found him a towel and a complete change of clothes, and plied him with coffee strongly laced with brandy. Reid stopped shaking. Some color returned to his face, but even so he looked more exhausted than any man Tom had ever seen, a creature of skin and bone, kept on his feet by sheer willpower.

Tom wanted to put Reid to bed with a hot brick—but he could imagine the major's affront if he made such a suggestion.

He took Reid down to the salon and gave him a plate piled high with macaroons, and once Reid had eaten them all he sent him back to Marlborough in Lucas's curricle, a groom sitting up behind him.

"How do you think he is?" Tish asked, once Major Reid had gone.

Tom looked at her anxious face and thought that Reid would be mortified if he knew she was worried about him. "He's perfectly well. Stop fussing, Tish. It'd take more than a toss to upset a man like Reid!"

Chapter Fifteen

November 18ᵗʰ, 1808
Whiteoaks, Wiltshire

Sir Henry Wright left the next day, and Tom was sorry for it, because he liked the man. Wright didn't seem downcast by Tish's refusal of his proposal; on the contrary, his grin was wider than ever and there was a buoyant spring in his step.

"He took it well," he said to Lucas. Unlike Stapleton, who'd been as sullen as a penned bull.

He and Lucas rode over to the folly, and climbed the ruined tower and kissed, and he said, "Do you want my hand or my mouth," and Lucas chose his hand, as he always did. Some days were rough and fumbling and hasty, others slow and intense. Today was the latter: a long, leisurely build-up, gently stroking, stroking, stroking, until Lucas was moaning low in his throat and their cocks were hot and damp and desperate in his hand, and when Lucas begged breathlessly,

"Oh, God, now, please, *now*," he tightened his grip and pumped hard, and they both climaxed, bucking helplessly.

Tom caught their seed in his handkerchief, and they stayed leaning against each other for long minutes, the smell of sex musky in the cold air—and then they straightened their clothes and went down to the courtyard and Lucas posed as Sir Gawain—feet apart, shoulders back, holding an old rapier—and Tom painted him.

He hummed as he worked, and it was pleasant to be here with Lucas, just the two of them and the easel and the paintbrushes, but he found himself dissatisfied, too. He didn't want to paint Lucas as Sir Gawain; he wanted to paint him as Atlas, as Samson, as Hercules, as Ajax Telamon. On canvases eight feet high, in oils. And he wanted to paint Lucas naked, the full glory of his body revealed: the muscular arms, the powerful thighs, the taut buttocks.

But in those paintings he'd hide Lucas's cock, block it with shadows or a fold of cloth, angle his body so it was out of sight. That cock—the Ox—was his alone. If he ever painted it, it would be only for himself to see.

Tom imagined setting up his easel, laying out his brushes, choosing the colors for Lucas's cock. Carmine, definitely, and vermilion and madder red. A hint of smalt for the strong veins. Orpiment for the golden nest of hair. And when he had everything ready, he'd get down on his knees and suck Lucas until that massive cock was thick and suffused and straining—but he wouldn't let Lucas climax; he'd paint him instead.

Shit, he was hard himself, now. Achingly hard. He wanted Lucas's salt on his tongue, wanted to inhale his scent, wanted the hot, sharp taste of Lucas's seed.

He hadn't had Lucas's cock in his mouth in weeks, not since that first time in the dungeon.

Tom looked at the watercolor, and he looked at Lucas, and then he laid down his brush and crossed to where Lucas stood.

"Is my arm wrong?" Lucas asked.

"No," Tom said, and he caught Lucas's chin in his hand and kissed him.

Lucas made a muffled sound of surprise, and then he dropped the rapier and kissed Tom back.

"This time I'm not giving you a choice," Tom said, when they broke for breath. "*I* get to choose."

"What?" Lucas said, and then, "Tom . . . no . . ." as Tom knelt, and then after that Lucas didn't say anything coherent for quite some time.

THE AFTERNOON PASSED LEISURELY, peacefully. Tom let each color dry before laying down the next, and while he waited, they lazed in the cool, winter sun and Lucas told him about the estate he'd inherited in Cornwall, describing the old stone house, the fields with their crooked walls, the bright blue sea. "The bailiff's teaching me how to manage the farm," Lucas said. "I know this'll sound stupid, but . . . I really enjoy it."

"It doesn't sound stupid." Tom could easily imagine Lucas as a gentleman farmer, tramping over fields all day, mud caking his boots, wind tousling his hair, sun tanning his face. And he could just as easily imagine Lucas in the evenings, sitting quietly by a fireside reading.

"It's different when it's your own place, y' know?" Lucas said, plucking grass blades. "There's nothing for me to do here, but at Pendarve it's all mine. I want to do the best I can."

"Of course you do." Tom climbed to his feet. "I'd like to see Pendarve."

"Next month," Lucas said. "I promised Robert I'd stay for his birthday—he's a bit prickly about turning forty—but we can go straight after that."

Tom mixed the next color, and thought of the sketchbook with the musket ball buried in it. A sick feeling grew in his belly. *What if these three months are all the time we have? What if I never see Lu again after this?*

That thought sat at the back of his brain for the rest of the day, as persistent as a damned horsefly. He found himself aware of seconds winging by, minutes slipping past—time that he would never again share with Lucas. At four o'clock he packed up his color box. There wasn't much left to do—a few shadows that needed deepening, some glints of sunlight in Sir Gawain's hair.

They rode back together slowly, enjoying each other's company without needing to talk, but Tom's awareness of time passing persisted. It was as if he had an hourglass at the back of his skull and he could hear the whisper of each sand grain falling.

They dismounted in the stableyard. Tom wanted to hook his arm around Lucas's neck and pull him close for a kiss, right there, in front of the grooms. He turned away and unstrapped his painting kit from the saddle and went upstairs to his room.

A letter was waiting for him, propped on the mantelpiece.

Tom stared at it, and felt the same sense of doom that he always felt before a battle.

He ignored the letter while he washed, while he changed for dinner, but once those tasks were accomplished he could no longer postpone the inevitable.

He picked up the letter and reluctantly broke open the seal. The message was brief: General Wellesley required him back in London to give his testimony.

Tom placed the letter back on the mantelpiece, then he went down to dinner and spent the evening pretending that he wasn't desperately in love with his best friend.

Chapter Sixteen

November 19th, 1808
Whiteoaks, Wiltshire

WHITEOAKS WAS SLOWLY EMPTYING, his brothers, sisters, cousins and their assorted spouses, children, nursemaids, abigails, and valets departing. When Bernard told him he was leaving that morning, Lucas suppressed a silent *Thank God*. When Tish told him she was leaving, too, he felt the opposite emotion. "Must you?"

"Yes," said Tish. "Come to the library; I need to talk with you."

"Sounds ominous," Lucas said. "Should I be worried?"

Tish didn't reply. She led him briskly to the library, closed the door, and stood with her back to it, her eyes intent on his face. "How are you?" she asked bluntly.

Lucas gave an inwards flinch. He fixed a smile on his face. "Never been better." He strolled to one of the tall windows.

Tish followed him. "Truthfully, Lucas. How are you?"

"Never better," Lucas said firmly, looking out at the winter-bare rose garden. "Do you think it will rain? I hope not. That painting's still not quite finished."

"Lucas, the *truth*."

He turned his head and looked at her, still smiling. "I told you—"

"I can hear when you're lying."

Lucas's smile froze. He looked away, out the window. Memories slid over one another in his head like a deck of cards being shuffled—and halted at one he'd long forgotten: Tish the day after her twenty-first birthday, eager to show him and Julia a new trick she'd learned: how to tell truth from lies.

He hadn't believed it. Julia hadn't believed it. They'd spent two hours trying to prove that she was wrong, that it was impossible—but Tish had caught every lie he and Julia had attempted. Every single one.

And then she'd never mentioned it again, and that memory had been buried by a thousand others.

"So you can still do that trick?" he said, finally.

"Yes." Tish took his hand and interlaced their fingers. "Truthfully . . . how are you?"

Lucas stared out at the gray clouds, the leafless rose bushes, the raked gravel paths, and thought about Julia, and how much he missed her. "I've been better," he said finally. "But don't worry about me, Tish. It takes time, is all."

"Is there anything I can do to help?"

Lucas smiled at her. It came out lopsided. "No, love. But thank you."

Tish didn't release his hand. "I'm glad Tom's back."

"So am I."

"Does it help?"

Lucas thought about how Tom made him feel: the terri-fying mix of panic and elation, the sense that his life was spinning out of control. Should he say *Yes*, or *No*? Both would be the truth.

But that wasn't what Tish meant; she was asking about Julia's death.

"It helps a lot."

Lucas stared out at the winter landscape and tried to find a word for what Tom was to him. More than friend. More than lover. When Tom was with him, he no longer had the sense of having lost a limb. He felt whole again. Was there a word for that?

Savior. I think he's my savior.

With a sense of shock he realized he'd uttered those last words aloud: "I think he's my savior." God, how would Tish interpret that? Lucas laughed hastily and tried to make a joke of it: "Or perhaps my ruin."

And that was the truth. He and Tom were surely destined to be each other's ruin if they didn't halt this mad, dangerous affair.

Tish didn't return the laugh. There was a frown on her brow.

"Tish, don't worry about me," Lucas said firmly. "I'll be all right." And then he wondered whether that sounded like a lie to her, because he wasn't at all certain that he'd be all right once Tom left. It would be like Julia's death all over again. *Oh, God, how will I cope?*

Tish didn't look completely content with this answer, but she nodded and let go of his hand.

Lucas turned towards the door, glad the conversation was over. "When are you leaving?"

"At ten."

"I'm going to Cornwall next month." Lucas held the door open for her. "Tom hasn't seen Pendarve yet."

Tish halted in the doorway. Her expression was serious.

"Tish?"

"I love you," Tish said, her voice almost fierce. "And if there's ever anything I can do for you—*anything*—I hope you will tell me."

"Of course I will. Honestly, Tish, don't worry about me."

Tish stepped close and hugged him briefly. "Be careful!"

Lucas blinked. "I'm always careful." And then a shiver of premonition crawled up his spine. *Does Tish know about Tom and me?* He tried to look puzzled, not alarmed. "Tish? What's this about?"

"Nothing. Good-bye!"

Lucas stood in the doorway and watched her walk briskly down the corridor.

Tish didn't know. She *couldn't* know.

Chapter Seventeen

HE AND TOM RODE over to the folly once Tish had gone. They climbed the stone steps to the grassy courtyard; Tom glanced in the direction of the dungeon. "Later," Lucas said. "Let's get the painting finished first, in case it rains."

Tom looked at the sky and shrugged. He set the easel up.

Lucas stood in the familiar pose and tried not to worry, but the conversation with Tish gnawed at him. Tish *couldn't* know . . . could she?

The more he thought about it, the more certain he became that Tish *did* know—and that she'd been warning him to be careful.

It became difficult to stand still. His heartbeat was spiky with agitation. "Tom," he blurted finally.

"What?"

"I think Tish knows. About us."

When Tom painted, he had an expression of narrow-eyed yet slightly unfocused absorption, as if he was daydreaming and concentrating hard at the same time. That expression vanished now. "What? Nonsense!"

"She was asking about you—about *us*—and then she told me to be careful."

Tom stared at him for a moment, the paintbrush held in mid-stroke, and then shook his head decisively. "No."

"But—"

Tom put down the paintbrush and crossed to where Lucas stood. "Tish told you to be careful because she's worried about you. Everyone's worried about you." He cupped the back of Lucas's head in one hand, leaned close, kissed him lightly. "She doesn't know. No one knows. All right?"

"But—"

"Relax, Lu. She doesn't know."

Lucas closed his eyes and leaned into Tom. His agitation began to unravel. Tom was correct. Tish couldn't know.

Tom kissed him again—softly, gently, reassuringly—and stepped back. "Ten more minutes and I'll be done. All right?"

"All right."

Tom was good to his word. Ten minutes later he stepped back from the easel, surveyed the painting critically, and then said, "Finished. Come and have a look. Tell me what you think."

Lucas had been watching the painting grow for days, but there was a big difference between an almost finished painting and a finished painting. He peered closely, trying to determine what Tom had done in the past hour to make Sir Gawain stand out so vividly. "It's incredible. What did you do?"

Tom shrugged. "Mostly shadows and light."

Lucas examined the painting while Tom cleaned his brushes and packed away his painting kit. If he hadn't known that Sir Gawain was himself dressed in a tailcoat and breeches and with an old rapier in his hand, he would never have guessed it. This was Oscar—older and taller, but still unmistakably Oscar—wearing chainmail and a tabard and brandishing an impressive longsword.

"I don't know how on earth you do this, Tom. It's like magic." And then he hesitated. "Can I pay you for it?"

Tom snorted. "Don't be ridiculous."

"But you've spent *hours*—"

"I enjoyed it," Tom said. "I like spending time with you." He hesitated, and then said, "Wellesley wants me back by the twenty-second."

Lucas felt the smile drain off his face. "He's recalling you from furlough?"

Tom shook his head. "Just wants me to give testimony. Shouldn't take more than a day or two, and then I really should visit m' brother. I'll be gone ten days, two weeks at the most."

Lucas stared at him in dismay. Two whole weeks without Tom.

"And then we can go down to Pendarve. Just the two of us."

Lucas nodded, but the dismay didn't go away, because at the end of December, Tom would leave. And he wouldn't just be gone two weeks. He'd be gone months. Years. Maybe forever.

Tom glanced in the direction of the dungeon. His head tilted, asking a silent question.

Lucas's dismay stuttered to a halt.

Tom stood looking at him, his head cocked to one side, his lips quirked at the corners.

Lucas's throat grew tight. His heart thudded loudly.

"Now?" Tom said.

Lucas blushed, and nodded.

Tom laughed. "I love the way you blush, Lu." He took

Lucas's hand and tugged him towards the dungeon. "I'd like to paint you with oils," he said, as he led Lucas down the twisting stone staircase. "You're wasted as Gawain."

Coolness and shadows and privacy enveloped them. Lucas's heart began to beat faster in anticipation. The sound of Tom's name was loud in his head: *Tom, Tom, Tom.*

Tom pushed him firmly back against the wall, and stepped close, pressing the full length of his body against Lucas. "You should be Atlas," he whispered in Lucas's ear. "Or Samson."

Lucas tried to find a reply to this, but his mind was blank. All he could think of was how *good* it felt to have Tom pressed against him like this, thigh to thigh, chest to chest.

Tom didn't wait for a reply; he kissed Lucas, and it wasn't a soft, gentle, reassuring kiss. It was rough and hungry. Lucas's hips rocked involuntarily—and Tom rocked back—and Lucas didn't wait for Tom to ask him, just said, "Hand," hoarsely, and they both fumbled with their breeches. His whole body jolted when his cock touched Tom's, and jolted again when Tom's hand wrapped around them both.

They made love fast, frantically, biting each other's mouths, panting, groaning. The rhythm of Tom's hand was merciless and the sound of his name was deafening in Lucas's head: *Tom, Tom, Tom.* His climax was short, sharp, brutal, close to pain.

Afterwards, they stood leaning into each other in the cool dimness of the dungeon, their cocks nestling quietly in Tom's hand, and the feeling of intimacy between them was far greater than when they'd been straining together. Lucas rested his forehead on Tom's shoulder, closed his eyes, and felt the familiar urge to cry, felt the familiar conflicting emotions: panic and joy and shame, pure happiness counterbalanced by the sense that they were hurtling towards ruin. He wanted to say, *We have to stop this,* and at the same time, *Hold me forever.*

Tom sighed, and opened his hand.

Lucas opened his mouth to say, *Don't*, and managed to swallow the word. He fumbled with his drawers, with his breeches.

"Uncle Lucas? Uncle Tom?" The voice was young and female, echoing in the stone stairwell. "Are you down there?"

Tom recoiled away from Lucas as if the words had been a musket shot.

"Uncle Lucas?" This time Lucas recognized the voice: Selina, Robert's eldest daughter. Riding boots clattered on the steps.

Tom hastily crossed to the other side of the dungeon.

Lucas shoved his shirt-tails into his breeches.

"There you are!"

Selina appeared around the bend in the stairway, her sister Emma behind her, and behind them, Emma's governess.

Shit, shit, shit, whispered a panicked voice in Lucas's head. Were his breeches properly fastened? His shirt fully tucked in? He didn't dare look down and find out.

"What are you doing down here?" Selina asked brightly.

There was a thin, sharp, terrible pause, and then Tom said, "I thought it might make a good backdrop for a painting, but it's too dark."

Selina skipped down the last of the steps. "Do you think so?"

No, no. Go back up. Selina and Emma wouldn't recognize the faint, musky odor of sex, but the governess might.

"Dramatic, but too gloomy," Tom said, at the same time that Lucas blurted: "Tom finished Sir Gawain. Did you see it up there?"

"Yes," said Selina. "It's *divine.*"

"Will you paint us, too, Uncle Tom?" Emma asked shyly.

"Emma," the governess reproved in a quiet voice.

"Maybe," Tom said. He moved towards the staircase and made an ushering movement with his hands, like a farmer's wife trying to herd geese. "When's your birthday?"

To Lucas's utter relief, they yielded to Tom's urgings, turning and heading up the stairs again. "February," he heard Emma say. "And Selina's is in August."

Tom followed on their heels.

Lucas stayed where he was, listening to the receding echo of voices and scuff of feet. His heart was pounding against his ribs, his lungs clenched as tightly as fists. Awareness of how close they'd come to disaster reverberated in his head. If Selina had come down the steps earlier, if she'd not called out . . .

What fools they'd been, reckless and careless and unmindful of danger, thinking they were safe when they weren't.

He pressed the heels of his hands to his eyes. To be almost discovered by Robert's *children*.

An unforgivable thing to do to Selina and Emma, to Robert, to Almeria. He and Tom would have *deserved* to be ruined.

Lucas lowered his hands and opened his eyes and took a deep breath. *This stops now.*

He started for the stairs—and stepped on something soft. The handkerchief Tom had used to catch their seed.

"Christ," he said, under his breath. He picked it up— crumpled and damp and smelling of sex—and shoved it in his pocket.

Chapter Eighteen

THEY ALL RODE back to Whiteoaks together, Lucas and Tom, the girls, the governess, the groom who'd accompanied them. Lucas stayed as far from Tom as he could. He conversed with the governess in awkward, stilted sentences. Did she know what she'd almost stumbled upon? By the time they reached the stableyard, he was fairly certain she didn't.

They'd been lucky. Undeservedly lucky.

He dismounted and gave his mount to a groom.

"Lu," Tom said.

"Not now," Lucas said, brushing past him. *Not now. Not ever again.*

He climbed the stairs to his bedchamber fast, and stripped off his riding clothes. His hands were shaking. "Pantaloons and Hessians," he said to Smollet. "The bronze green tailcoat. And a fresh neckcloth, please." No more riding alone with Tom. No more trysts. Why did that make him want to cry? He'd known all along that what he was doing was wrong and dangerous and stupid. *I should never have let him come here with me.*

He dressed in the clothes Smollet brought him. It took three tries to tie the neckcloth. His damned fingers wouldn't stop trembling.

He gave up on the Mail Coach and tied a Barrel Roll instead, then shrugged into the tailcoat and looked at himself in the mirror. A little too pale, a little too tense.

"Are you all right, sir?" Smollet asked.

"Perfectly," Lucas said. "Never better."

He was in the green and gold salon, sipping tea and eating macaroons with Robert and Almeria, trying to pretend that he hadn't nearly brought disaster down upon his whole family, when he remembered the handkerchief. He choked on his tea, put the cup down in its saucer with a clatter, and pushed to his feet. "Forgot something!" he blurted, and hurried from the salon.

Lucas took the stairs three at a time, half-ran down the corridor, burst into his room.

Smollet wasn't there.

He went hastily through his clothes, found the tailcoat he'd worn riding, groped in the pocket. The handkerchief was gone.

Lucas closed his eyes. *Shit.*

After dinner, when Tom said, "Lu, we need to talk," Lucas didn't try to brush him off. He went with Tom to the library.

Neither of them sat. Lucas was too tense. The meal he'd forced himself to eat sat uneasily in his belly.

Tom said, "Look, Lu, about today," at the same time that

Lucas said, "Do you have your crest on your handkerchiefs?"

"What?" Tom said.

"Your handkerchiefs. Do you have your crest on them?"

Tom's brow creased. "No. Why?"

"Because Smollet found that handkerchief you used today. I put it in my pocket—and I forgot it was there—I should have rinsed it out, but I didn't—and Smollet *found* it!"

Tom stepped forward and laid a hand on Lucas's arm. "Lu, he's not going to wash it himself. The laundry maid—"

Lucas jerked free and retreated two steps. "We have to stop. We have to stop *right now*."

Tom lowered his hand.

"It doesn't matter who washes the damned thing. Smollet *found* it, and he'll know it's not mine, and it *smells* of us." He heard his voice, heard the panic in it.

"Lu, you're overreacting—"

"It's not just the handkerchief! Robert would never forgive me if his daughters had seen us—and he'd be *right*."

Tom grimaced faintly, and Lucas read that expression as agreement.

"Tom, we have to stop this. You *know* we have to stop this." He took a deep breath. "I think it's best if you don't come back after seeing your brother."

Tom physically flinched. "What?"

Lucas looked away from his face. "I don't think you should come back."

There was a long moment of silence, and then Tom said stiffly, "What about Pendarve?"

Lucas shifted his gaze, met Tom's eyes. "I'm sorry."

Tom stared at him for a long moment. His eyes were bright and hard, his mouth tight. He turned on his heel and walked stiffly across the library and shut the door behind him with a short, sharp *click*.

Chapter Nineteen

LUCAS LAY AWAKE that night and thought of all the ways in which he'd been a fool. Finally dawn came. He climbed out of bed and dressed, responding to Smollet's comments with monosyllables, unable to look the man in the face. Then he went down to breakfast and stared at his plate without eating anything. And then Tom left.

Almeria was talking about an excursion to Bath, and Robert about the hunting season, but the words were just blurred sounds in Lucas's ears. He excused himself and went up to the farthest nook of the vast attic, a place he'd come to often in the weeks after Julia's death, the only place at Whiteoaks where he could be certain of being alone.

Fool, fool, a thousand times a fool.

He sat in the same shadowy corner he'd sat in so many times before, drew up his knees, rested his head on them.

The familiar sense of having lost a limb was back. Not just Julia gone, but Tom, too.

At least up here there was no one watching him. No one to hear him cry.

THE NEXT DAY, Smollet placed a folded square of white fabric on Lucas's dressing table. "Master Tom's handkerchief," he said. "Should I have it sent to him, or will he be back?"

Lucas's brain was dull from lack of sleep. The cogs turned slowly—processed Smollet's words—and jammed to a halt. "I beg your pardon?"

"Master Tom's handkerchief."

For several seconds his tongue refused to work, and then he managed to say, "Tom's?"

"It has his initials, sir." Smollet carefully laid three starched neckcloths over the back of a chair. "Will he be back?"

"No," Lucas said.

Initials. No crest, but *initials*.

"That's a shame, sir. It does you good to have him here." Smollet held the fourth neckcloth out to Lucas.

Lucas took it, and turned to the mirror. What the devil had Smollet meant with that comment?

Maybe he doesn't know?

He placed the neckcloth around his throat and fumbled with the folds. Of course Smollet knew. It wasn't just the handkerchief. His clothes had probably been reeking of sex for the past six weeks.

His eyes winced shut. Mortification was cold on his skin, cold in his belly. *Smollet's known the whole time.*

"Sir?"

Lucas opened his eyes and stared at the neckcloth. It was a mess. He stripped it from his throat.

Smollet selected another neckcloth and held it out to him.

Lucas took it numbly, looped it around his throat, attempted a Barrel Knot.

"Perhaps you could invite Master Tom to Pendarve, sir? Before he leaves England."

His gaze jerked to Smollet's reflection in the mirror. The man's face was as bland as his voice had been.

Lucas looked back at his neckcloth. The shape he'd tied made no sense to his eyes. It wasn't a Barrel Knot. It wasn't anything.

He unwound the neckcloth. Smollet handed him a fresh one.

This time, Smollet kept silent while Lucas tied the neckcloth. He helped Lucas into his tailcoat—claret red today—and then said, "Will there be anything else, Master Lucas?"

"No, thank you."

Smollet picked up the three neckcloths—one still pristine, two needing starching and ironing—and departed.

Lucas stayed where he was, staring at the mirror.

Perhaps Smollet hadn't smelled sex on his clothes. Perhaps he hadn't noticed the semen in the handkerchief.

And perhaps pigs will grow wings and fly.

Chapter Twenty

TOM TRAVELED BY mail coach from Marlborough.

Late on the twentieth, he arrived in London.

On the twenty-first, General Wellesley was subjected to a lengthy examination, from which he came away as cross as a bear.

On the twenty-third, Tom gave his own evidence at the Royal College in Chelsea, in front of four generals and three lieutenant generals.

He told the truth: That after the victory at Vimeiro, Wellesley had been as mad as fire to pursue the French. That he'd urged an advance in no uncertain terms. That he'd protested against the conditions of the preliminary armistice. That he'd signed it unwillingly and only because a superior officer desired him to do so. That he'd had no part in negotiating the final convention.

Afterwards, he asked Wellesley if the general wished to rescind his leave.

"I've enough people under my feet," Wellesley said sourly.

"Don't need you, too." And then his face relaxed into something close to a smile. "Thank you, Lieutenant, for what you said in there. I appreciate your loyalty."

On the twenty-fourth, Tom got drunk on cheap brandy. Halfway through the bottle, his rage fizzled out and he found himself weeping.

On the twenty-fifth, he woke with a sore head.

On the twenty-seventh, he departed for Yorkshire to visit his brother.

Chapter Twenty-One

December 2nd, 1808
Whiteoaks, Wiltshire

LUCAS COUNTED THE days until he could leave. Three weeks until Robert's birthday. Two weeks. Ten days.

When he had one week left, he came down to the salon, dressed for dinner, and found only Robert there. "Almeria and the girls are dining over at the Thorpes', so it's just you and me tonight." Robert clapped him cheerfully on the shoulder. "Come and have a drink in my study. I told them to put dinner back an hour."

Lucas followed his brother into the candlelit study. A fire burned in the grate, flanked by leather armchairs.

"Brandy?"

Lucas nodded.

Robert poured him a generous glass. "Sit, sit."

Lucas sat.

He sipped in silence while Robert talked about the hunter

he'd just bought—strong hocks, good movement—the new phaeton he had his eye on—a high-perch, and perhaps too dashing for a man of his age?—and the house he was hiring in London for Selina's début—in Grosvenor Square, with a ballroom large enough to hold five hundred.

Finally Robert ran down. He refilled their glasses, sat in silence for a moment, and then said, "Lucas?" The tone of his voice was different, not heartily cheerful but quiet, almost gentle.

Lucas glanced at him.

"Look, I know it's none of my business, but . . . did you and Tom have a row?"

Lucas looked away, at the fire. "No."

"When's he coming back?"

"He's not."

Silence drew for a moment, broken only by the hiss and crackle of the flames in the grate, then Robert said, "That painting he did of Oscar, it's as good as any in the long gallery. He's wasted in the army. Do you think . . . he'd consider selling out?"

"No."

"Does he like it that much?"

"No." And then, because Robert's question seemed to require a more elaborate answer, he said, "He can't afford to sell out."

"Ah," Robert said, and then after a moment, "If it's a question of money—"

"I already offered. He won't take charity." Lucas drained his glass and set it down.

Robert poured again. "Almeria's not here to tell us off if we get a bit bosky," he said, with a wink.

Lucas dutifully smiled.

"You know . . ." Robert said, and then hesitated.

Lucas sipped the brandy. It was doing its job. Everything was becoming slightly hazy around the edges.

"You know," Robert said, again. "When I was younger, I used to envy you, having a twin."

Lucas halted in mid-sip. His gaze jerked to Robert.

"Hugh and I never got along that well—still don't, truth be told—he gets so damned sanctimonious—and I used to look at you and Julia and . . . wish I had a twin, too."

Lucas lowered his glass.

"And then you went to Eton, and the first time you came back for the holidays you brought Tom Matlock with you, and I envied you him, too." Robert shook his head, pulled a shamed face. "I had scores of friends, and you had just one, and you were only eight years old, but even I could see that your friendship with Tom had more substance than all of mine put together."

Lucas looked down at his brandy. He didn't know what to say.

"I used to think you were lucky, having Julia and Tom. But you're not. Because if you're that close to someone and they leave you, you never get over it."

Lucas's gaze was unwillingly drawn to Robert again.

His brother's expression was more serious than he'd ever seen it. "We've been worried to death about you, Lucas—and then Tom came back and you were happier—and now he's gone again, and you're not talking—"

"I talk," Lucas said stiffly.

Robert lifted his eyebrows. "How many words have you spoken today?"

Lucas thought about it. "Not many," he admitted.

"You're not talking," Robert repeated firmly. "And you're hiding up in the attic again, pining yourself half to death."

Lucas clutched his glass. "You know about the attic?"

"This is my house, Lucas. If one of my guests is up in the attic every day, of course I know about it."

Lucas looked down at his brandy.

Robert was silent for a moment, then he sighed. "You're not like Almeria and me. You enjoy the balls well enough, but what you'd really prefer is a quiet evening with perhaps one or two people. Am I right?"

Lucas hesitated, and then nodded.

"Emma's like you. I don't know if you've noticed. It worries me sometimes. I think she'll find her first Season difficult."

Lucas glanced at his brother.

"You like solitude, and you only let a few people close to you—and there's nothing wrong with that, Lucas—but it means that if those people leave you . . ."

Lucas looked hastily back at his glass. A lump was growing in his throat. *For God's sake, don't cry.*

"I don't think I've ever been as lonely as you are right now," Robert said quietly.

Lucas squeezed his eyes shut. *Don't cry.*

Robert got up and attended to the fire. He took his time stirring the embers with the poker, selecting a fresh log, laying it precisely. By the time he turned back, Lucas was able to meet his eyes with composure.

"You remember Uncle George and John Wallace?"

Lucas stiffened.

"You and Tom remind me of them."

Lucas opened his mouth to deny this, but his tongue was frozen.

"I'm not saying you should live in each other's pockets if you don't want to—but if Tom *does* want to sell out and it's just a question of money—"

"He won't take charity."

"Who said anything about charity?" Robert sat again and reached for his glass. "Julia had quite a bit of money. *I* don't need it. *You* don't need it."

Lucas processed this statement. "You mean . . . a bequest?"

"A bestowal. All Julia's money came to me; I can distribute it as I see fit." Robert sipped slowly, his eyes on Lucas's face. "You knew Julia best. How do you think she'd feel about giving some of it to Tom?"

The answer to that question was easy. He could practically *feel* Julia's approval. His imagination told him that she was leaning over his shoulder, whispering in his ear, *Tell him I like it, Lu!* He even smelled her perfume for a few seconds—bergamot—and then the scent faded. Lucas blinked twice, and swallowed hard, and said, "She would have liked it."

"And what about you? Would you like it?"

That was a harder question. Did he want Tom to sell out?

He thought of the musket ball buried in Tom's sketchbook. *Yes*. And then he remembered that moment in the dungeon: Selina and Emma almost finding them.

Lucas twisted his glass round and round. "I don't know."

Robert leaned forward. "Lucas."

Lucas reluctantly met his eyes.

"I couldn't do anything about Julia's death—no one could—but I'm damned if I'm going to watch you go through this again. Not if it can be *fixed*."

Lucas looked away. *It's not as simple as you think.* Thoughts revolved agitatedly inside his skull. He gulped a mouthful of brandy. Another mouthful. "Did you ever wonder," he blurted, and then stopped.

"Wonder what?"

Lucas gripped his glass tightly. "If Uncle George and John Wallace were . . . were . . ." The word *lovers* choked in his throat. His gaze skittered to the fireplace, to one candelabrum and then the other, and lastly, unwillingly, to Robert's face.

Robert was watching him, his eyes disconcertingly shrewd. "Back door ushers?"

Lucas couldn't control his flinch—or his grimace of revulsion.

"If they were, they were discreet." Robert sipped his brandy. "Sophia said she saw them holding hands once, in the shrubbery. I never quite believed her—she was always making up stories—pixies in the garden, ghosts in the folly—but Hugh believed her. He ran and told Mother, and Mother gave him a deuce of a scold." He chuckled into his brandy.

"Scold? Why?"

"For telling tales. Or maybe it was for spreading gossip. I don't remember which. But I *do* remember she said that if her brother and John Wallace were holding hands, it was no one's business but their own, and she was right." Robert shrugged, and drank the last of his brandy. "Hugh didn't agree, but he's always been a bit of a prig."

Lucas turned his glass in his hands. "I don't remember that."

"You were still in the nursery."

Lucas stared down at the reflections in his brandy. He remembered Selina's voice floating down the stone stairwell, her quick footsteps, her bright-eyed face, her question: *What are you doing down here?*

Robert wouldn't be chuckling into his brandy if his daughters had come down those stairs five minutes earlier.

"So, it's settled?" Robert said. "I'll have a bank draft drawn up."

Yes. No. I don't know. He looked at Robert in an agony of indecision.

Robert huffed out a sound that was half laugh, half sigh,

and shook his head. "Almeria always said that Julia did the talking for you both, and you did the worrying, and she was right. She's usually right." He reached over and gripped Lucas's shoulder and shook him lightly. "Stop worrying, young clunch. And drink that brandy. Dinner's in five minutes."

Chapter Twenty-Two

December 6th, 1808
Riddleston, Yorkshire

When his father died Tom had been in the final week of his final term at Oxford. The funeral hadn't been memorable, but the interview he'd had afterwards with his brother would live in his memory forever—the full extent of their father's debts, the choice Daniel had given him: the clergy or the army. It wasn't the words themselves that he remembered, but rather the tone of Daniel's voice, the halting way he'd spoken. Daniel had apologized—*apologized*—as if the fault was his and not their father's.

Tom had been relieved the crushing burden hadn't fallen on him—and ashamed of himself for being relieved—and guilty that he'd been able to escape and Daniel hadn't.

He still felt guilty.

Daniel had sold the town house in London and the hunting lodge in Leicestershire. He'd sold carriages and horses, jewelry and paintings and silverware—and it hadn't come close to clearing the debt.

He'd kept Riddleston Hall—shabby, leaking, centuries old —and the farms that comprised the Riddleston estate. The hall was exactly as Tom remembered it from his last visit, but the farms were much improved and Daniel himself not so careworn. "It's looking good," Tom said, after they'd spent an afternoon riding around the estate.

"The yield's tripled," Daniel said, leaning down in the saddle and closing a gate behind them. "It's finally bringing in good money. I think—I *hope*—we'll see our way clear within the next fifteen years."

Fifteen years seemed a long time to Tom. "That's good," he said, and felt the ever-present guilt.

Daniel smiled cheerfully. "We had a stroke of luck— Hetty's aunt died and left her some money. Enough to enclose the last of the fields—and *fix* the roof. I don't know if you remember how it used to leak—"

"I remember."

"Well, it doesn't anymore."

They trotted along the lane, round the bend—and there was Riddleston Hall, a rambling half-timbered manor house of russet brick.

Daniel slowed, and halted.

Tom reined in alongside him.

"The next two years' profits will go back into the farms," Daniel said matter-of-factly. "After that, we'll start repairing the hall. There's a lot needs doing."

Tom thought of his bedroom—curtains so faded there was no telling what color they'd once been, carpet threadbare, ceiling stained with damp, bedsheets so thin he'd put his foot through one last night.

"Hetty's making lists—order of importance. Kitchen first.

If we're careful, we'll get it all done in five or six years. Then a Season for Amabel and one for Chloe, and after that . . . Another seven years, I think. Maybe less, if the yield continues to increase." Daniel didn't look bowed down; he looked optimistic.

"I'm sorry I can't help," Tom said.

Daniel smiled at him. "You have helped. You've never once asked for money, and I know it can't be easy."

Tom felt himself flush with embarrassment. Daniel thanking *him*? "It's not that difficult." Each time he received his pay, the choice was simple: alcohol, or sketchbooks; gambling, or pencils; whoring, or watercolor cakes. Easy.

Daniel shrugged as if he didn't quite believe him and then said, "I hope you know that if you ever find yourself in trouble, you can ask for help."

And dig you deeper into debt? "Thank you," Tom said, even more embarrassed. "But I'm twenty-seven; I can look after myself." *And I'd rather sell my painting kit than ask you for money.*

"Sometimes the unexpected happens." Daniel's gaze returned to the hall. His lips thinned, not in bitterness, but in determination. "I'm going to leave my boys more than debts and a ramshackle estate. By the time Hetty and I are finished, this place will be worth inheriting. Harry and Lawrie won't let it fall to rack and ruin again." His face relaxed into a smile, his pride in his sons clear to see. "They're good lads. Got Hetty's common sense. Very steady."

Tom heard the silent addendum: *Not like Father.*

They eased into a slow trot, along the lane, down the long drive, across the forecourt, around to the back.

The Whiteoaks stableyard was a bustling, noisy place, grooms hurrying about their work, scores of horses—hunters, riding hacks, carriage horses. The stableyard at Riddleston was modest, quiet, shabby. Tom dismounted and handed his horse to the single groom.

"Letter just came for you, sir. Express it were."

"Express?"

Tom hurried inside. Did General Wellesley need him?

But the letter had come from Wiltshire, not London, and the handwriting, that tidy black copperplate, was as familiar to him as his own messy scrawl was.

All his anger, his hurt, came flooding back.

"Not bad news, I hope?" Daniel said.

Part of him—the angry part—wanted to screw the letter up without reading it. The hurt part was hoping for an apology.

Tom hesitated, and then slid his thumb under the wax seal.

Lucas's letter was very short.

I'm sorry. Will you please come to Pendarve with me?

Tom stared at those words. An apology, but not enough of one—and an olive branch.

He didn't want pages of contrition and pleas for forgiveness, he just wanted three extra words: *I'm sorry. I love you. Will you please come to Pendarve with me?*

"Bad news?" Daniel asked again.

But Lucas is never going to tell me he loves me, is he?

Tom sighed, and refolded the letter. "No. Good news, actually."

Chapter Twenty-Three

December 14th, 1808
Whiteoaks, Wiltshire

TOM ARRIVED CLOSE TO DUSK. Lucas followed Robert into the great entrance hall to greet him. Tom looked weary and travel-stained, his neckcloth limp, his coat creased, his jaw unshaven. Their eyes met. Tom gave a nod. A curt nod, not a casual, friendly nod.

"Glad to see you again," Robert said, shaking Tom's hand. "Heard the news yet?"

"What news?"

"You won't believe it! None of us did. But I'll let Lucas tell you. Make yourself at home, Tom." He clapped Tom on the shoulder, and headed back to his study, his footsteps brisk.

Lucas and Tom looked at each other.

Emotions warred in Lucas's breast—joy and sheer relief at seeing Tom again—and fear, because all the reasons he'd asked Tom to leave still existed. The drumbeat was loud in his head: *Tom, Tom.* He wanted to step towards Tom and hug him, heedless of the consequences—and he wanted to stay where he was and tell Tom that this had been a mistake and that Tom should go.

The moment lengthened, both of them silent. Tom's lips were compressed and there was no merriment in his eyes.

He's still angry with me. And regret joined the churning mix of emotions in Lucas's breast. Regret that he'd angered Tom, that he'd hurt him, because the last thing in the world he wanted was to hurt Tom.

"Thank you for coming." He offered the words awkwardly, diffidently.

Tom gave another short nod. "What news?"

"A letter from Tish." Lucas fished it from his breast pocket and held it out.

Tom unfolded the letter and read swiftly. His eyebrows came together in a frown, and then climbed his forehead. He glanced at Lucas, as if for confirmation.

"She's married your major. The announcement was in the newspapers today. Letitia Trentham and Icarus Reid."

Tom looked back at the letter and read down to the bottom. "Tish and Reid," he said, when he'd finished. "My God." If he'd been angry before, he wasn't angry now. He looked bemused, a little worried.

"She's asked us to visit her on the way to Pendarve. I looked it up—Woodhuish—it's not far out of the way. I thought we could . . . if you want to?"

"Yes," Tom said. "I do." He handed the letter back. "Tish and Reid. My God."

"I'll send Smollet ahead to Pendarve." Lucas nervously turned the letter over in his hands. "You and I can travel by post-chaise. Four days down to Devonshire, see Tish, then on to Pendarve." Having uttered the words, he felt a spurt of panic. Alone. With Tom. And on the heels of panic was a stab of longing so intense that it *hurt*.

Tom's eyes focused on him. He was no longer thinking of Tish and Major Reid; his attention was fully on Lucas.

The drumbeat in Lucas's head became louder. "If . . . if you wish?"

Tom thought about it for a moment, and then nodded. Not a curt nod.

"Thank you for coming," Lucas said again, almost a whisper.

This time, when he said it, Tom smiled at him. Not one of his wide, merry smiles—a small, lopsided smile, half sad, half wry—but it was still a smile.

The painful stab of longing came again and the drumbeat grew even louder, and counterpoint to those things was fear. *We will be each other's ruin.* Lucas clutched the letter and literally trembled with the strength of his conflicting emotions.

Chapter Twenty-Four

December 15th, 1808
Whiteoaks, Wiltshire

THEY LEFT WHITEOAKS close to noon and stopped for the night at a posting inn just south of Grovely Wood. The post-chaise—spacious, clean, well-sprung—was a vast improvement on the mail coaches Tom had spent the last three days in, but in every other respect the journey was disappointing.

Lucas's words yesterday had given him hope: Smollet sent on ahead, just the two of them in the post-chaise. He'd imagined them kissing, touching, maybe indulging in some hasty sex—but he'd known within half a minute of climbing into the carriage that there would be no kisses, and definitely no sex. Lucas was tense, radiating *Don't try to touch me* as strongly as if he'd said the words aloud.

Tom sat alongside Lucas for thirty miles and stewed with frustration. Rain drummed on the carriage roof. Three times he opened his mouth to have it out with Lucas, and three times he stopped himself. *Wait until we're out of the post-chaise and he doesn't feel so cornered.*

Seen in the dusk and the rain, the posting inn was a dour place, but inside it was unexpectedly pleasant. The private parlor was cozy, the meal first-rate, and the wine surprisingly decent. Lucas relaxed fractionally, but everything about him still said *Don't touch me.*

Tom, whose mood had mellowed with the wine and the food, found himself growing cross again. After the covers were removed he leaned back in his chair and sipped the last of his wine, waiting, not saying anything. Tension gathered between them, a *frisson* that reminded him of the night he'd kissed Lucas in the Brook Street Mews—the air seemed to bristle with expectancy, with anticipation.

He finished his wine and put the empty glass on the table. Lucas glanced at it, and seemed to become tenser. Tom waited a moment, then pushed back his chair. Lucas's gaze fixed on him. He reminded Tom of an unbroken horse, apprehensive, ready to bolt.

Tom stood. "I'm going to bed," he said, and waited for Lucas to say something, *anything.*

But Lucas didn't speak; he just sat there, looking tense. Tom saw the conflict on his face—the shame, the longing.

Out with it, Lu. Ask me to spend the night with you. But it became clear that Lucas wasn't going to say it, and he was damned if he was going to be the one who always pushed, the one who always begged. "Good night," Tom said, and turned away from the table.

He paused at the door and looked back, giving Lucas one last chance.

Lucas was standing, and he looked so miserable that Tom relented. "Coming upstairs?" he said.

Lucas hesitated, and then nodded.

They climbed the stairs together, and halted in the corridor outside their rooms. Tom said nothing, just waited, and after a long moment, Lucas opened the door to his bedchamber.

Tom followed him inside and closed the door and locked it.

The room wasn't large. The bed dominated the space, a four-poster with piled-up pillows and a blue counterpane.

Lucas went to stand by the little fireplace, looking taut and nervous.

Tom halted in the middle of the room. *Ask me to spend the night with you, damn it.*

Silence grew between them, but it wasn't a silence filled with anticipation, it was a silence filled with anxiety—and that wasn't how sex should be, wasn't what he wanted.

"You know what?" Tom said flatly. "Let's not do this." He turned and walked back to the door.

"Tom . . ."

He halted with his hand on the door handle, and looked at Lucas. "If you want something from me tonight, you're going to have to tell me what it is, because I'm not Julia and I can't read your damned mind."

But that was a lie. Anyone would be able to read Lucas's mind right now; his inner torment was clear to read on his face.

He wants me to stay the night with him, and he hates that he wants it, and he can't bring himself to ask for it, and if I walk out this door, he's probably going to cry.

Tom's anger fell away. He sighed, and crossed to where Lucas stood, and pulled him into a hug.

Lucas flinched slightly, and then leaned stiffly into the embrace. He was trembling.

"It's all right, Lu," Tom said, and he pressed his face into Lucas's hair. "It's all right."

Lucas relaxed by slow increments. His shoulders lost their stiffness. His head bowed. His forehead rested on Tom's shoulder.

"Do you want me to stay with you tonight?"

"Yes," Lucas whispered.

Chapter Twenty-Five

IT TOOK THREE more days to reach Woodhuish, and they were good days. And good nights. But not great, because while Lucas allowed the sex to happen, participated in it, enjoyed it, slept in Tom's arms afterwards, Tom was aware of an invisible and insurmountable barrier between them: Lucas's shame.

He couldn't imagine Lucas ever initiating sex between them, saying in an urgent voice, "Tom, I need you *now*," just as he couldn't imagine Lucas joking about what they did. Lucas would die rather than say "Get your saber out, Tom, and let's have a swordfight."

He'll be glad once I'm gone. Glad when this is over.

For some reason, that made him both angry and sad. He wanted to hit something, and at the same time wanted to cry.

He stared out the window at the Devonshire countryside—gray, damp—until he'd mastered both those urges, and then looked over at Lucas, dozing in the far corner of the post-chaise.

Why did I have to fall in love with you?

He might as well ask why the sun rose in the east each morning. The answer was the same: Because it was meant to be. It had been impossible to not fall in love with Lucas all those years ago. Just as it was impossible not to love him now.

He fished his sketchbook out of his pocket and drew Lucas. If he ever had the occasion to paint an archangel, he'd use Lucas as the model—that golden hair, the symmetry of his face, the perfect blend of beauty and masculinity. And the purity.

Tom lowered his pencil and looked at Lucas. He should have painted Lucas's face on Sir Gawain. Lucas was Sir Gawain made flesh: chaste and pure.

Until I corrupted him.

He remembered the night of Lucas's birthday, remembered what had happened in the Brook Street Mews. Two times when he could have turned away—two times when he'd chosen instead to cross that line.

Lucas probably wishes I hadn't.

Tom sighed, and closed the sketchbook and slipped it back into his pocket. Every time he came home on leave he'd be faced with that choice again—and he'd make the same decision again—and have to break down Lucas's resistance again.

But it would be worth it, because Lucas was worth it. Quiet, private, tidy, steady, good-hearted Lucas. Lonely, grieving Lucas. Lucas who *deserved* to have a lover, who deserved intimacy and moments of physical ecstasy, who deserved to fall asleep being held by someone who loved him —even if those things brought him as much shame as pleasure.

Tom reached over and took Lucas's hand.

Lucas stirred, opened his eyes, smiled sleepily.

Tom felt his heart lurch in his chest, as if the post-chaise had run into a pothole. He smiled back, and tightened his grip on Lucas's hand. *I love you. I will always love you.*

TISH HAD WRITTEN that she would be staying at Woodhuish House with a Lady Ware, whom she described as a newfound cousin. The closest inn was three miles away, the Golden Hind. From the outside it was the most painstakingly clean country tavern that Tom had ever seen—fresh whitewash, scrubbed doorstep, no grass daring to grow between the cobblestones.

The innkeeper was as neat and scrubbed as his inn—and massive, taller than Tom, broader than Lucas. *If I ever paint Goliath, this is the man.* He had the deformed ears and scarred eyebrows of a man who'd had a career in the ring. His name suited him: Mr. Strike.

Tom looked at Mr. Strike's humorless face and thought, *Lu and I need to be careful while we're here.* This was a rigid, exacting man. A man who would pay attention to what his guests did.

He revised his opinion when he saw the chambermaid. She brought them hot water, then lingered in the corridor, flirting. There was nothing demure about the assessment she gave them both—head to toe—or the offer that followed that and the saucy flick of her skirts as she headed back down the stairs.

Tom watched her out of sight. Why would he want a woman, however pretty and willing, when he had Lucas? "The innkeeper's not such a stickler for propriety as I thought. Not if he hired her."

"Did she mean what I think she meant?" Lucas said.

"I think it's pretty clear what she meant."

"But . . . *both* of us? At the same time?" Lucas looked so shocked that Tom laughed.

"You're such an innocent, Lu. Yes, both of us at the same time. I'd swive her, while she, er, smoked your cheroot. Or the other way around."

Lucas digested this statement, an expression of distaste on his face. "Have you ever—?"

"No." Although he'd once spent a memorable afternoon in bed with two women—but he didn't think Lucas would like to hear that tale.

"Smoke a cheroot? Is that what you call it?"

"It's what Armagh sometimes called it, when he was joking." Tom saw the colonel in his mind's eye, grinning, saying *I feel like smoking a cheroot, Lieutenant, and yours is the closest.*

Lucas's face stiffened, as it always did at mention of Armagh.

Tom turned his head away to hide a smile. It was foolish, but he liked Lucas's jealousy. It told him Lucas didn't want to share him with anyone. He pulled out his pocket watch. "Too late to visit Tish today."

HE SPENT HALF the night in Lucas's bed—among other things, smoking Lucas's cheroot—before creeping back to his own room. He fell asleep thinking of Lucas—and woke worrying about Tish and Major Reid. But when he saw them three hours later, at Woodhuish House, he stopped worrying. Tish hadn't married Reid out of pity, and Reid hadn't married her for her money. They were in love. Tish looked so luminous that his fingers itched to draw her, and Reid was unrecognizable as the man who'd visited Whiteoaks.

Tom hugged Tish and shook hands with Reid. "Lord,

Major, you've put on at least a stone! Tish been forcing you to eat?"

Reid glanced at Tish, laughter in his eyes.

Tish went pink. "Not any longer."

The last remnants of Tom's worry evaporated. This was the man he'd served with. Too thin still, but alive in a way Reid hadn't been in Wiltshire. There was ease in Reid's body and contentment in his smile. The damage that had been done to him in Portugal was mended.

He and Lucas ate luncheon at Woodhuish House with Tish's new cousin, Lady Ware—petite, blonde, pregnant—and her husband, Sir Barnaby.

"What do you think?" Lucas asked afterwards, when they were riding back to the inn on the hacks they'd hired.

"A good match," Tom said, without hesitation. "Reid's strong enough not to let her boss him, and they're clearly, uh . . ." He searched for a polite way to say *having great sex.* "Compatible." He wasn't certain what made it so obvious— something in the way Tish and Reid had looked at each other? Whatever it was had been as unmistakable as it was indefinable, and it made him think about sex, about naked skin and sweat and heat and panted breaths. It made him want to tumble Lucas into bed, even though it was only mid- afternoon.

He was pretty confident that Lucas was thinking about sex, too, that the prickling, humming sense of anticipation between them wasn't just his imagination, and when they dismounted in the stableyard he was proven correct. Lucas scuffed the toe of one boot on the clean cobblestones and said diffidently, "Want to come up to my room for a bit? We could, um, play cards?" And then he met Tom's eyes and blushed so vividly that Tom was glad the ostler had already turned away.

"Yes," Tom said. "I do."

The pretty chambermaid met them on the stairs, and brushed against Tom's arm so that he felt her soft breasts.

Tom almost laughed. *Nice try, love, but I have a much better offer.*

He followed Lucas into his room, locked the door, and leaned against it. Lucas crossed to the table and picked up the pack of cards and stood fidgeting with it, still blushing, looking awkward and self-conscious and hopeful and shy all at the same time.

Tell me what you want, Lu.

He knew what *he* wanted. Lucas's fat, rosy cock in his mouth. Nothing could match the intense intimacy of it, the way Lucas filled all his senses. He loved the salty taste of Lucas's skin and the bitter taste of his mettle. Loved the faint musky scent of his sweat. Loved the size of him, the smoothness, the hardness, the heat. Loved the sounds Lucas made, the helpless groans, the way he shuddered and trembled.

Tom straightened away from the door. "Forget the cards," he said, taking the pack and tossing it on the table. "Take everything off."

Chapter Twenty-Six

THEY STRIPPED OFF THEIR CLOTHES. Lucas's fingers fumbled with haste. *Tom, Tom, Tom.* They kissed greedily, urgently— Tom's cock burned against his belly, almost branding him— and then they were on the bed, rolling over one another, almost wrestling, kissing fiercely, their mouths hard, hot, hungry.

He found himself on his back. Tom broke the kiss, panting, and sat up. Lucas tried to sit up, too, but Tom shoved him back down and bent and captured Lucas's cock in his mouth.

"No," Lucas said, and grunted as Tom sucked hard. His balls tightened, and his hips twitched helplessly, and then he said, "No," again more loudly, and sat up and grabbed a handful of Tom's hair, pulling his head up.

They stared at each other, both breathing heavily. Tom's pupils were dilated, his cheeks flushed, his lips glistening.

"I don't want that," Lucas said. He didn't want to lie back and be passive while Tom smoked his cheroot, or whatever that bloody colonel had called it. He wanted to be *active*. He wanted Tom straining against him, hips grinding together, mouths biting, cocks clashing.

He clenched his fingers in Tom's hair and hauled him closer and kissed him even harder than before, and then they were wrestling on the bed again, limbs tangling, mouths tangling, tongues tangling, and now Tom was on top, and now he was, and then they rolled right off the bed, and Tom said, "Oof," when they hit the floor.

"You hurt?" Lucas said.

"No."

He rolled Tom onto his back, pinned him with the weight of his body, and bit the curve where Tom's shoulder met his throat, dragging his teeth roughly over the skin, sinking them into the muscle.

Tom gasped, and jolted convulsively.

"Like that?" Lucas asked, and licked where he'd bitten.

"God, yes."

Lucas bit him a second time, even harder, and Tom jolted again, his body bucking helplessly.

Lucas bit his way down Tom's torso, not gently, but roughly, his teeth leaving marks. He bit Tom's pectorals, his nipples, bit the lean sheet of muscles that covered his ribs, and every time Tom tried to twist away, tried to sit up, he shoved him back down. He could smell Tom's arousal, smell sweat and muskiness, and the smell made the drumbeat in his head even louder. *Tom, Tom.*

He bit Tom's taut belly, and licked where he'd bitten, and Tom's cock was right there, inches from his mouth, and he could *smell* it, could feel its heat like a small furnace, and he almost turned his head and took it in his mouth—but panic fluttered in his chest, and he hesitated, and reached down and took Tom's balls in his hand instead.

Tom jerked at his touch, and hissed out a breath. "Careful."

He was careful—careful, but rough—handling Tom's balls as he would his own, stroking, squeezing, tugging, while Tom breathed in short, fast gasps, almost whimpering, his body twitching helplessly and his cock—the Corinthian—straining, and leaking, and growing a deeper shade of red than Lucas had yet seen it.

His own cock ached and throbbed in sympathy. He knew he couldn't last much longer. Knew neither of them could.

Lucas let go of Tom's balls and captured the Corinthian instead. It was damp and desperately eager—and part of him wanted to bend his head and discover what that slick helmet felt like beneath his tongue, discover what it tasted like, and part of him shrank from doing so.

He tightened his grip and pumped once, hard.

Tom's hips lifted off the floor. A guttural sound came from his throat.

Lucas pumped again—and again—and again—rough and hard and fast—and Tom bucked and panted and uttered incoherent noises—and Lucas pumped again, even more roughly, and leaned over Tom and sank his teeth into the muscle where Tom's shoulder met his neck.

Tom jackknifed on the floor. His cock jerked in Lucas's hand, hot semen spurting, and Lucas's cock jerked in unison and his whole body spasmed, great jolts of pleasure that rolled through him repeatedly.

When the jolts had faded to tingles, Lucas released Tom's cock and stretched out alongside him.

Neither of them said anything for a long time, and it felt good to be lying here on the floor with Tom, sated and weary.

"Fuck," Tom said finally, hoarsely. "I think you just about

killed me." He sat up with a groan, moving stiffly, as if every bone in his body ached.

Lucas's contentment vanished. Shame filled the space where it had been. He sat up, too. "Did I hurt you?"

Tom looked down at his chest and abdomen. Lucas saw the sticky spattering of semen—and the red marks where he'd bitten him.

"I'm going to have bruises," Tom said ruefully.

Lucas averted his gaze, too ashamed to look at him. *I did that. Me. I fucked him on the floor and bit him until he almost bled.* He felt sick, sick to the pit of his stomach. "I'm sorry."

"Sorry? What on earth for? That was the best sex I've ever had in my life."

Lucas's gaze jerked back to him.

"When you bit me that last time, my skull just about exploded."

"You . . . liked it?"

Tom laughed. "Lu, I've had sex hundreds of times. Hundreds and hundreds of times. And that was the best. *Ever.* Yes, I liked it."

"Oh," Lucas said. He felt himself blush. The shame was gone. Instead, there was a warm feeling in his chest that he didn't quite recognize, as if he was pleased and proud at the same time.

Chapter Twenty-Seven

Tom sat on the floor, gathering the strength to stand. At least it was a clean floor. He felt half-drunk, a little dazed. Pleasure still reverberated in his bones, like a bell long after it had been struck. Who would have thought Lucas could make love like that? Fierce and dominant.

It's going to work between us. He knew it with certainty. Lucas had almost initiated the sex, and he'd certainly controlled what they'd done. It wouldn't be too many days before he was asking for what he wanted, instead of diffidently suggesting card games.

He turned his head and looked at Lucas, sitting on the floor alongside him, magnificent in his nudity. He reached over and hooked an arm around Lucas's neck, pulled him close, kissed him high on the cheek. "I love you."

Lucas didn't say the words back to him. He tensed, a flinch, almost a recoil.

And just like that, Tom's sense of half-drunk pleasure was

gone. Hurt and anger came rushing in to take its place. He released Lucas and climbed stiffly to his feet.

He kept his head turned away from Lucas, found his handkerchief, wiped his chest clean, started dressing. His ribcage was tight and his movements jerky and his eyes stung and he was so *angry* with Lucas, angry with him for having sex like that—unbridled and passionate on the floor—and then rejecting him. Because that's what that stiffening had been: a rejection. It had been Lucas saying *I don't want your love.*

Lucas stood and began dressing, too, silently.

Drawers, stockings, breeches. Shirt, waistcoat, neckcloth. Tom sat to pull on his boots, stood to shrug into his tailcoat, and still neither of them had spoken. The air in the bedchamber was brittle. They both knew he was angry, and they both knew why.

Tom shoved his gloves in his pocket, picked up his hat, and crossed to the door. The key made a quiet *snick* as he turned it.

"Tom?"

Tom halted, and squeezed his eyes shut for a moment, and blew out a short, sharp breath, and turned to face Lucas. "What?"

Lucas hadn't put on his boots or his tailcoat. He stood in stockinged feet, holding a piece of paper in both hands, and he was six foot two and built like a prizefighter, and yet somehow he managed to look uncertain and shy and awkward and unhappy.

"What?" Tom said again.

Lucas turned the paper over in his hands, hesitated, and then laid it on the table, pushing it towards Tom. "This is for you."

Whatever it was that Lucas had laid on the table was an apology; that was blindingly clear. Everything about Lucas was apologetic—the angle of his head, the set of his shoulders, even the way his hand pushed the paper—and it was clearest of all in Lucas's voice. He'd said "This is for you," but underneath that, clearly audible, was *I'm sorry I upset you.*

Tom stayed where he was for several seconds, wrestling with his anger, with his hurt, and then he pressed his lips together and walked back to the table. "What is it?" He put down the hat, picked up the paper—and froze.

For a moment his eyes refused to believe what they saw. It was a mistake. It had to be a mistake. He'd misread it. It didn't say—couldn't possibly say—what it did.

He read it three times. Four times. And each time it said the same thing.

Thirty thousand pounds. Thirty *thousand* pounds.

His brain stuttered to a halt for several seconds—and then leapt into action, galloping in several directions at once. *Thirty thousand pounds.* He could sell out. He could give half to Daniel, more than half—two thirds—and he'd *still* have a small fortune. He could afford to paint in oils. He could buy a curricle. Hell, he could buy a *house.*

He looked at Lucas, now watching him warily, and then back down at the bank draft.

He wanted it. God, he *wanted* it.

His heart was beating fast, and his fingers trembled slightly, and he felt a little light-headed—and beneath those things, was hot, bitter rage.

Tom put the bank draft carefully back on the table. "I told you I don't want char—"

"It's not charity. It's not my money. It's Julia's."

Tom stood with his mouth half-open while his rage collapsed inwards on itself and the rest of his sentence congealed on his tongue. Julia's money.

"It was Robert's idea. Not mine. But he asked me about it. He wanted to know what Julia would have thought."

Tom closed his mouth.

"I told him she'd want you to have it. Because I know she would."

Tom swallowed. Christ. Thirty thousand pounds. He picked the bank draft up again. His fingers trembled more strongly than they had before.

"You can sell out," Lucas said, his voice diffident, as if afraid of giving offense.

Tom glanced at him. "You want me to?"

Lucas hesitated, and then said, "It's safer."

Safer. That wasn't what he'd wanted Lucas to say. He wanted him to say *Yes, please, because I love you and I can't be without you.* Which was stupid, because Lucas would never say that. Lucas would rather cut out his tongue than say that.

He looked at the bank draft. Julia's money. Robert's idea. And then he looked at Lucas standing awkwardly on the other side of the table. "You'd prefer it if I didn't sell out, wouldn't you?"

Lucas hesitated again. "No."

The hesitation lasted less than a second, but it hurt even more than the flinch had. Tom's anger flamed to life again. "You'd prefer it if I went away and never came back, wouldn't you? If we never did that again." He gestured at the bed, at the floor. "Wouldn't you?"

Again, Lucas hesitated.

"Fuck you," Tom said fiercely. "And fuck your money." He threw the bank draft down on the table, wrenched the door open, and flung himself out into the corridor.

He went down the stairs fast, so angry he was crying. Or maybe the tears weren't from anger, maybe they were because Lucas had hesitated, and that had been like a kick in the chest and it damned well *hurt*.

Chapter Twenty-Eight

TOM WALKED HALF a mile down a hedged-in Devon lane, striding fast, propelled by rage, dashing tears from his eyes, furious with himself for crying, furious with Lucas for making love on the floor and then flinching, for giving him that bank draft and then hesitating. Thirty *thousand* pounds.

And then the rage drained away, leaving a bitter ache in his chest, and he just felt tired and sad.

He halted, and looked around, and saw a spinney with tangled brambles and a dark-leaved holly and the trunk of a fallen oak.

He crossed to the oak and sat, his elbows on his knees, and stared at the ground, at rotting leaves and winter-dead grass and withered twigs.

The more he stared at the leaves and grass and twigs, the more certain he became that he'd overreacted.

Yes, Lucas had flinched, and yes, Lucas had hesitated—but he'd also made love on the floor, and he'd given him thirty thousand pounds, and he wanted him to sell out because it was safer.

I shouldn't have told Lucas I love him. Tom closed his eyes and rested his head in his hands. God, what a *stupid* thing to do.

Lucas didn't want his love. Lucas would much rather *not* have his love, because Lucas thought that a man loving another man was something to be ashamed of—and that was never going to change, because that was who Lucas was.

He opened his eyes and stared down at the dead leaves. *I want too much from him. I want more than he can ever give me.*

The leaves were a dozen different shades of brown, like swatches at a tailor's: drab and tan and nankeen, snuff and cinnamon, Dust of Ruins and Paris mud. He watched a millipede crawl over a dark brown leaf that a tailor would call carmelite and thought about the bank draft, about Lucas wanting him to sell out because it was safer.

And then he thought about Daniel and Hetty and what twenty thousand pounds would mean to them.

And then he stopped thinking about the bank draft and just thought about Lucas. Lucas punching him two months ago—Lucas sleeping in his arms last night—Lucas rolling him off the bed today. *He's given me his trust and his body. It's not fair of me to want more from him. He's doing the best that he can.*

But he did want more. He wanted Lucas not to flinch when he told him he loved him. He wanted Lucas to say the words back to him.

And he knew it was never going to happen.

Tom sighed, and rubbed his face, and climbed wearily to his feet. He owed Lucas an apology.

DUSK WAS GATHERING in the sky by the time he reached the

inn. He halted, and took a moment to think through what he was going to say to Lucas.

Movement caught his eye: the pretty chambermaid hurrying across the stableyard, her skirts gathered in one hand. Her hair was disheveled beneath her mobcap, her bodice askew, and she had an exultant little smile on her face. She looked exactly like a young woman who'd just indulged in a quick and enjoyable swive. Tom watched her slip back into the inn, and then looked down at himself. He spent a minute checking his buttons, straightening his cuffs, smoothing his lapels, and half a minute combing his hair with his fingers. Thank God the neckcloth hid the bite marks on his throat. When he was certain he didn't look like a man who'd recently had bedsport with his lover, he took a deep breath, crossed the yard, and pushed open the door.

The sound of an argument echoed in the Golden Hind.

"I didn't! I swear I didn't!" The voice was the chambermaid's, high-pitched and tearful.

Caught by her employer, Tom guessed, and trying to lie her way out of it. He didn't like her chances, not with that crooked bodice and her hair falling out from underneath the mobcap.

He grimaced, and headed for the stairs. *Good luck, love.*

"He made me do it! I didn't want to!" She was crying now, noisily.

Tom set his foot on the first step, and glanced into the taproom. Yes, as he'd suspected: a weeping chambermaid and a grizzled Goliath of a landlord, fury on his face, a fist the size of a blacksmith's sledgehammer half-raised.

Tom hesitated. *He's not going to hit her, is he?*

"He made me!" the chambermaid cried, and she looked wildly round, and pointed at Tom. "It were him! He *made* me do it!"

Tom took his foot off the step. "What?"

The landlord swung round. His head hunched slightly into his shoulders. He looked like a bull about to charge.

Tom held his hands up, placatingly. "I can assure you that—"

The landlord came at him, fist raised.

"I didn't—"

He tried to duck, but the landlord was faster than he was. He heard his nose break. *Crack.*

Everything went black for a moment, and then awareness came rushing back, and along with it, the most agonizing pain Tom had ever experienced in his life. He was on the floor again. Second time today. Through watering eyes, he saw the landlord standing over him, and behind him the chambermaid, tear-streaked and horrified. Her mouth was open—she was screaming—but he couldn't hear it. His ears were ringing too loudly.

He opened his mouth, but no words came out. Blood poured from his nose, choking him, and he couldn't say *Wait a minute,* or *It wasn't me,* couldn't say anything at all.

Chapter Twenty-Nine

Lucas pounded heavily on the door to Woodhuish House. When the butler opened it, he almost fell inside.

"Tish—Miss Trentham—Mrs. Reid—where is she? I need to see her!"

The butler took a step backwards.

"It's an emergency, man. *Where is she?*"

"Mrs. Reid is in the blue salon—"

Blue salon? Wasn't that where he and Tom had sat with Tish? Lucas pushed past the butler and half-ran down the corridor to the right. This door? No, this door. He burst into the room. "Tish!"

Six people were in the blue salon, and they all started at his entrance.

"Tish, I need your help. You have to come! Now!"

Tish stood. "Lucas? What's wrong?"

"Now!" he said frantically, almost crying.

Major Reid stood, too, and so did everyone else, and if it wasn't so urgent he'd be mortified.

Tish took his hand. "Lucas, what's wrong?"

"It's Tom," he said, and now he *was* crying. "The landlord's half-killed him, and he's in the roundhouse, and they said he attacked the maid, but he *didn't*—he *wouldn't*—and I need you to do that thing with the lies—I need you to tell them that he's *innocent!*"

"Of course he's innocent," Tish said, gripping his hand tightly. "I'll come."

"Strike hit him?"

Lucas looked at the man who'd asked the question, and his brain identified him: the Earl of Cosgrove. "Yes. Tish, you have to come *now*."

"I'll come, too," Major Reid said, and Lucas didn't really care, as long as Tish came *now*.

"And I," said Cosgrove. "The constable knows me. Is your friend hurt badly?"

"Yes."

"Then I'm coming, too," said the pretty, and very pregnant, Lady Ware.

"No," Sir Barnaby said.

"No," Cosgrove said, too. "We'll bring him to you." And it made no sense to Lucas, but he didn't *care*, as long as Tish came.

"Hurry," he said urgently. And everyone hurried.

THE ROUNDHOUSE WAS IN KINGSWEAR. It took half an hour to get there, Lucas on the horse he'd hired, Tish and Reid and Cosgrove following in a carriage. Moonlight glinted on the wide, black River Dart.

The constable did indeed know Lord Cosgrove. "My lord," he said, with a respectful nod.

"Evening, Davies," Cosgrove said. "I understand you have Lord Riddleston's brother in your custody."

The constable looked blank. "Who?"

"Lieutenant Matlock. Lord Riddleston's brother. He's injured, I believe."

Lucas opened his mouth to say *Let us see him now!* but Reid touched his arm lightly and gave a little shake of his head.

Lucas bit back the words and waited in an agony of urgency while Cosgrove and the constable conversed. Cosgrove was polite and pleasant. He pointed out that Tom was a nobleman's son and that the roundhouse was perhaps not the best place for him, particularly if he was injured. He offered to assume responsibility for Tom's custody until such time as the charges could be proved true or false.

Davies hesitated, and fetched a lantern.

The roundhouse was a stone building no larger than a closet, with a domed roof and a thick, oak door. The constable unlocked the door, his keys jangling. Lantern light spilled inside, creating jerky shadows, showing the single wooden bench and the man sprawled on it.

Lucas shoved the constable aside. "Tom?"

The roundhouse smelled of fresh blood, and beneath that, of old vomit and stale sweat and urine. Tom looked worse than he had an hour ago. His eyes were swollen shut, his face a mask of dried blood. He was breathing hoarsely through his mouth, and blood bubbled in his nose with each breath.

Lucas knelt. "Tom?" If he didn't know it was Tom, he wouldn't have recognized him. "Tom?"

But Tom didn't stir, even when Lucas gently shook his arm.

Someone came to stand alongside Lucas. He glanced up and saw Tish, white-faced, and Lord Cosgrove. Cosgrove didn't look pleasant anymore; he looked grim. "How long has he been out for?"

"Uh . . . nearly two hours now."

Cosgrove turned to the constable. "Do you wish to explain to Lord Riddleston how you allowed his brother to die in a roundhouse?"

After that, it went swiftly. The constable produced a hurdle, and a horse and cart. With the help of the coachman and a footman, Tom was carefully loaded onto the hurdle and then into the cart. He still didn't stir. He lay as limply as if he were dead.

"A blanket," Cosgrove said, and the footman ran to fetch a blanket from the carriage.

Lucas laid the blanket over Tom, tucking it around him—and noticed Tom's right hand for the first time. It looked as if someone had trodden on it with hobnailed boots, piercing skin and snapping bones.

"His hand!" he said, aghast.

Reid gripped his shoulder. "He'll be all right."

"He needs a doctor!" Tom would think broken fingers a thousand times worse than a broken nose.

"Leave it to me," Cosgrove said, climbing up onto the cart seat and picking up the reins. He gave Reid a short nod. "You'll see to the rest of it?"

"We will."

Chapter Thirty

LUCAS WANTED TO stay with Tom, but he climbed into the carriage with Tish and Reid and the constable and went to the Golden Hind instead. The horse he'd hired trotted wearily behind on a long line. He sat gripping his hands tightly together, his right leg jittering, his heel drumming a fast, jerky rhythm on the floor, *tap-tap-tap*. He forced himself to stop the movement. *Tom's going to be all right.* But he wasn't sure he believed it.

"It was his right hand," he said. "He's right-handed."

Tish slipped her arm through his, and laid both her hands over his. "He's going to be all right, Lucas."

His foot was tapping again. "What if he can't paint again?"

"Lucas, don't borrow trouble." Tish leaned her cheek against his shoulder.

He tried to breathe calmly, tried not to tap his foot, tried not to worry—and after ten interminable minutes, the carriage drew up at the Golden Hind. They all climbed out.

The landlord, Strike, was in the taproom with his tapster and half a dozen customers. One of Strike's eyes was swollen shut. When he saw Lucas, a belligerent expression settled on his face. He stood up with slow deliberation.

Lucas matched him stare for stare. *I'll blacken your other eye for you if you dare to come closer.*

Silence spread through the taproom.

"Er, evening, Mr. Strike," the constable said, and nervously cleared his throat. "I'd like another word with that young lass."

Strike's eyes narrowed and his brows drew down. He opened his mouth—and saw Tish, and closed it again.

"In the coffee room," the constable said, and made another nervous throat-clearing sound. "We'll wait in there."

They repaired to the coffee room and took seats. Strike joined them a minute later with the chambermaid. She had lost her pretty pertness; she was pale and tear-stained.

"Sit down, Alice," Strike told her, not unkindly. "I won't let 'em bully you."

The maid sat. Her gaze flicked anxiously from face to face, and settled on the constable.

The constable cleared his throat again, and opened his mouth—and Reid said, "Alice? That's your name, is it?" His voice was quiet and his smile kind. "We'd like to ask you about what happened today."

The constable closed his mouth.

"She's already tole it once," Strike said, glowering.

"I would like to hear it for myself."

"And who are you?"

Reid was unintimidated by Strike's size and hostility. He met Strike's eyes, let several seconds pass, and then said, "Major Reid." He turned his gaze back to the chambermaid. "Is it correct that Lieutenant Matlock attacked you today, Alice?"

The maid hesitated, and kneaded her hands together, and cast a scared glance at the landlord.

"You don't need to tell me the details, Alice. Just yes or no."

The girl twisted her hands. "I don't know 'is name."

"If it was the man who was taken to the roundhouse, it's Matlock. Lieutenant Matlock. Did he attack you?"

The chambermaid squeezed her hands together until her knuckles turned white, and glanced at Strike again, and blurted, "Yes, sir."

Reid looked at Tish.

Tish shook her head.

Reid turned his attention back to the maid. He surveyed her for several seconds, and then spoke to Strike. "Mr. Strike, would you mind giving us a few moments' privacy?"

"I ain't goin' nowhere," the landlord said, folding his massive arms across his chest. "I know what you're up to—you'll give 'er money, and yon varmint will get off scot-free. Well, it ain't happenin'. Not in *my* inn, it ain't. Them as does wrong ought to be punished!"

Reid looked at Strike, and gave a faint shrug. "Very well." He brought his gaze back to the maid. "Alice, my wife has exceptional hearing. So exceptional that she can hear when people tell lies."

The maid's gaze jerked to Tish.

"Please tell me again . . . did Lieutenant Matlock attack you today?"

Lucas watched the chambermaid, watched her eyes dart from Tish's face, to Reid's, to Strike's. The silence lengthened. Ten seconds passed. Twenty seconds. The maid's expression grew desperate.

"Did *any* man attack you today, Alice?" Reid asked gently.

The girl's gaze fastened on him. Tears filled her eyes. She shook her head.

The constable stirred in his seat. Strike didn't merely stir, he pushed to his feet and lifted one meaty hand.

"Mr. Strike," Reid said quietly.

Strike lowered his hand. "Get out," he told the maid, his voice vibrating with rage. "I won't have your sort workin' here, whorin' and lyin'. Get your things an' get out."

The maid stood, tears sliding down her cheeks. "I'm sorry for what happened," she told Reid. "I didn't want to lose me job." She turned to the door, looking small and miserable, and if Lucas hadn't seen Tom lying on the hurdle with his face smashed and his hand smashed, he'd have felt pity for her.

Tish stood, too. She held out her hand to Reid. Reid seemed to understand the silent message. He handed her his pocketbook.

Tish followed the maid from the room.

Silence fell. Strike was still standing, red-faced and belligerent.

"Did you ask Lieutenant Matlock for his side of the story?" Reid asked.

"No." The landlord pushed his chin out. "Didn't think I needed to, not after what Alice tole me."

Reid sighed, and stood. "Mr. Strike, I agree with you: those who do wrong should be punished. But next time, send for Mr. Davies. Don't undertake the punishment yourself."

Strike's gaze fell. His chin lowered.

"You're damned lucky you didn't kill Matlock," Reid said. "His brother's an earl and he'd have made certain you went to the scaffold."

Strike glanced at Lucas.

Lucas stared coldly back. He had even less sympathy for Strike than he had for the chambermaid.

"Yon bruiser stopped me," Strike said. "Knocked me out cold." He nodded at Lucas, and there was apology in the dip of his head. "I'm right sorry, I am." And then he left the coffee room.

LUCAS WENT BACK to Woodhuish House with Tish and Reid, his and Tom's portmanteaux strapped to the back of the carriage. He stared out the window and thought of Tom. Tom's ruined face. Tom's broken fingers.

Lord Cosgrove met them in the entrance hall. "Sorted?"

"Yes," Reid said.

"How's Tom?" Lucas said urgently.

"Come and see."

They followed Cosgrove up the stairs and along a corridor. "Who attacked the maid?" he asked.

"No one," Reid said.

Cosgrove led them into a bedchamber—and there was Tom, tucked up in a four-poster bed. Sir Barnaby was leaning against one of the posts and Lady Ware sat holding Tom's left hand.

Lucas crossed to them hurriedly. "Has the doctor been?"

"Decided we didn't need a doctor," Sir Barnaby said. "Once we got all the blood washed off, it wasn't as bad as we thought." And it looked as if he'd been the one who'd done the washing off; he no longer wore a tailcoat, and his shirt-sleeves were rolled up to the elbow. "Take a look."

Lucas did.

Tom was still unconscious, but he looked better than Lucas had dared hope, far better, unbelievably better.

"The swelling . . ." he said, in disbelief.

"Cold compresses," Sir Barnaby said. "Worked wonders."

Lucas stared, incredulous. "His nose . . ."

"Not broken."

Not broken, not bleeding, not even swollen. There was a smudge of a bruise on the bridge of Tom's nose and his eyelids were a little puffy and shading towards purple, but those were the only signs that Strike had hit him.

Tom was six foot four, and yet he looked fragile lying in the big bed, his eyelids softly bruised, his lashes resting tenderly on his cheeks, his lips slightly parted.

"Has he woken yet?"

"For a few minutes. His wits aren't addled, if that's what you're worried about."

"And his hand? His right hand?"

Sir Barnaby leaned over and flipped back the bedclothes. "No broken bones. See?"

Lucas looked closely. Tom's right hand was a little bruised, and there were half a dozen scabs on the back, but that was all.

He released his breath in a trickle. "He's all right." He straightened, and turned to Tish, and felt tears prick his eyes. "He's all right."

Sir Barnaby clapped him on the shoulder. "He is. You hungry? I held dinner back."

THEY SAT DOWN to a very late and informal dinner: Tish and Reid, the Wares, Lord Cosgrove and his wife, and Lucas. Relief buoyed him through the first course—*Tom's all right*—but the second course was tainted by embarrassment. He'd burst into Sir Barnaby's house and dragged away his guests on an errand of urgency that hadn't been urgent after all. *They must think I'm a complete fool, that I saw the blood and panicked.*

His mortification grew as he picked at his syllabub. He recalled how he'd charged into the blue salon without being announced, how frantic he'd been. God, he'd even cried.

The ladies withdrew. The port and brandy were placed on the table.

"I apologize," Lucas said awkwardly. "For this evening."

"Forget about it," Sir Barnaby said, waving the apology aside with one hand. "You're Letty's cousin, and so are our wives—that makes us practically family."

"Thank you. For your help. All of you."

"You're welcome," Sir Barnaby said cheerfully. "Brandy or port?"

Cosgrove leaned back in his chair. "Reid tells me you gave Strike a black eye."

"Uh, yes."

"Right hook?"

"Yes."

"Knocked him out cold?"

Lucas nodded.

Cosgrove stared at him for several seconds, his expression difficult to read. Bemusement? Incredulity? Envy? And then he laughed, and shook his head. "You're going to be a legend in these parts, Kemp. Strike was in the ring for years and he was never—not once—knocked out. They call him the Invincible."

Sir Barnaby grinned. "Not any longer."

Cosgrove reached for his brandy and took a sip. "Used to see you at Jackson's Saloon a lot, didn't I?"

Lucas nodded. Cosgrove was an outstanding boxer; he'd often watched the man spar with Jackson. His mortification grew. *I blubbered like a schoolgirl in front of him.*

"Jackson once told me it was a shame you were so well-breeched, that you could have had a career in the ring. He said you had a right hook to watch out for."

"He was correct," Reid said dryly, "if you put that colossus down."

Lucas tried to smile. He gulped some brandy.

"How long are you staying?" Cosgrove asked. "Fancy a friendly bout?"

It should have made him feel better that all three men were politely ignoring the fact that he'd made a fool of himself, but it didn't. Lucas sat, and drank his brandy, and felt hot with humiliation.

Chapter Thirty-One

December 20th, 1808
Woodhuish, Devonshire

Tom woke to a headache and a feeling of tiredness. The clock on the mantelpiece told him it was nearly noon. He ate breakfast sitting up in bed—or maybe it was luncheon—and watched servants bring in a copper bathtub and fill it with steaming water.

The breakfast tray was removed. Tom climbed stiffly out of the four-poster. Lord, but he felt old today—old, tired, melancholy.

The bath helped a bit. He had a good wash, rinsing his hair over and over until it no longer smelled of blood. A manservant handed him a towel and offered to shave him. Tom accepted the offer; his right hand was clumsy today.

Once shaved, he dressed. Lucas's bite marks were visible, especially the one on his shoulder. Tom was too tired to care what the manservant thought.

He let the man tie his neckcloth.

"Please wait here, sir," the manservant said, once he'd helped Tom into his tailcoat.

For how long? But he couldn't be bothered asking.

He looked at his face in the mirror while he waited. Hadn't he heard his nose break? Obviously not. There was a faint bruise like a thumbprint high on the bridge, but other than that his nose was exactly the same as it had been yesterday, and the day before, and the day before that. That thumbprint and the shadowy purplish bruises under his eyes were the only sign that Strike had punched him.

He flexed his right hand, trying to ease the stiffness. He had no memory of hurting it. Had he hit Strike? It seemed unlikely, and it didn't account for the puncture wounds. He stared at the pattern the scabs made and came up with an answer: a hobnailed boot.

The manservant returned, with Sir Barnaby and Lady Ware.

"Good afternoon, Lieutenant," Lady Ware said, with brisk cheerfulness. "Please sit down."

Tom sat.

"How do you feel?"

"Very well, thank you," he said politely.

"No, truthfully."

"Tired," Tom admitted. "My head aches."

"Which part of your head?"

"My cheekbones, mostly."

Lady Ware spent several minutes examining him. She seemed to touch every part of his skull. Her hands were small and cool. When she'd finished, his cheekbones no longer hurt and his headache had receded. "And your right hand?"

"It's fine," Tom said. "Just a bit stiff."

She took his hand and felt her way along each bone, from

his wrist to the tips of his fingers. "Better?" she asked, when she'd finished.

"Yes," Tom said, and he wasn't just being polite. He looked at her curiously. "What did you do?"

"My wife has magic hands." Sir Barnaby said it as a joke, with a wink and a grin. "Come downstairs, Matlock. Your friends are anxious to see you."

HE WENT DOWNSTAIRS with the Wares. Tish and Reid and Lucas were sitting in a sunny parlor over the remains of their luncheon. They all stood hastily.

His awkwardness with Lucas was hidden in the chatter—Reid asking how he was, Tish teasing him that his eyelids were almost the exact shade of lilac as the gown she was wearing, Lady Ware suggesting a stroll down to Woodhuish Abbey to view the walled gardens, Sir Barnaby seconding the idea.

Lucas didn't say much. He seemed subdued.

Tom wished he and Lucas were alone so he could apologize for being such a cod's head yesterday. His moment came when they were out on the terrace.

"Lu, I'm sorry for what I said yesterday. I was out of line."

"Forget about it," Lucas said.

Apology given, apology accepted. He should have felt better, but he didn't. Maybe if he'd been able to take Lucas's hand and squeeze his fingers and feel Lucas squeeze back.

They stood for a moment together, not speaking. The silence between them wasn't quite comfortable.

"You still want to go to Pendarve?" Lucas asked, a little diffident, a little hesitant, as if he expected him to have changed his mind.

"Yes." At Pendarve they'd be able to talk privately and

maybe the sense that everything wasn't right between them would go away.

Lucas seemed to brighten. He gave a short nod. "I'll see to a post-chaise. If we leave first thing in the morning, we'll be there before dark."

Tom watched him hurry back into the house. He saw tomorrow unfold in his head: six hours in a post-chaise, and then they'd sit down to dinner together and afterwards, over brandy, they'd discuss the bank draft. Lucas would offer it to him again, and this time he'd accept it. And they'd pretend that he'd not told Lucas he loved him, and that Lucas hadn't flinched.

He sighed.

"You're looking very solemn."

He started, and found Tish standing at his shoulder.

"Where's Lucas gone?"

"Arranging for a post-chaise. Any moment now, a groom'll come trotting out of the stableyard, headed for Brixham." He smiled cheerily at her.

Tish didn't smile back. "Is everything all right?"

"Yes," Tom said, holding his arm out to her. "Walk with me?"

Tish slipped her hand into the crook of his arm. "What's wrong?"

"Nothing's wrong," Tom said firmly.

Tish's mouth tucked in at the corners. The glance she gave him made him uneasy, as if she didn't believe him.

Lucas returned, and they all set off—and Tom's suspicions were confirmed. Tish, normally a fast walker, lagged behind the others. Then, she stopped altogether. "A stone in my shoe."

But Tish didn't take off her shoe. She waited until the others were out of earshot, and then said, "What's wrong, Tom?"

"Nothing."

"Did you and Lucas quarrel?"

"Of course not."

Her head tilted to one side, as if she'd heard the lie in his voice. She looked at him for several seconds, her gaze narrow-eyed and assessing, and then appeared to come to a decision. "At Whiteoaks you told me your heart belonged to someone. It's Lucas, isn't it?"

Tom opened his mouth to deny this charge, but shock had stolen his breath.

"Isn't it?"

Tom forced a laugh. "No, of course not!"

"You lie terribly, Tom."

Tom closed his mouth. He had a plummeting sensation in his belly. *Shit. Shit.* His face felt cold, as if all the blood had drained from it. Tish *knew.*

But there was no condemnation on Tish's face, no disgust, no revulsion. She gave his arm a squeeze and said, "What's wrong, Tom?"

"Nothing," Tom said, and his voice sounded faint to his ears. "How do you know?"

"I saw you together at the folly one day."

Oh, Christ. Which day? What had they been doing?

"What's wrong?" Tish said again, and her voice held a note that said she was going to keep asking the question until she got an answer.

Tom looked down the valley, staring at the tree-covered slopes without seeing them, the long meadow, the great ivy-covered abbey where Lord and Lady Cosgrove lived.

"Tom?"

He took a deep breath. "He thinks it's wrong."

Tish didn't ask who *he* was, or what he thought was wrong.

Tom turned to face her. "If you make someone happy, if

189

you harm no one . . . how is that wrong?" There was frustration in his voice, or maybe it was anger.

Tish looked at him silently, and her expression was every bit as solemn as she'd accused him of being.

"Do *you* think it's wrong?"

Tish shook her head.

"Well, Lu does." The frustration drained away, leaving just a sense of defeat. "I wish . . ." *I wish Lucas was as open-minded as Armagh.* And thinking that—even for one second—was a betrayal of Lucas, and he felt ashamed of himself. "I wish things were different."

Tish squeezed him arm again, comfortingly. "You and Lucas are meant for each other, Tom."

"Lucas doesn't think so," Tom said bitterly. Ahead, the others had halted and were looking back. "Come on, Tish, let's catch up."

They walked briskly for half a minute, and then Tish slowed again. "He loves you, you know."

"No, he doesn't. He won't let himself." Tom kicked a stone. It skittered across the lane and buried itself in the grass verge. *How can loving someone be wrong?*

Tish didn't reply to this comment. She frowned instead.

Woodhuish Abbey was a beautiful building, centuries old, with arched windows and a crenelated parapet. Tom studied it as they drew closer. *One day I should like to paint it.* In the late afternoon, when the light was mellow. And he'd like to paint Tish and Reid, too. And he wanted to paint Lucas and Julia the way they should have been painted.

He glanced at Lucas, twenty paces ahead, walking with the Wares and Reid, and thought about how dissimilar Lucas and Julia had been—and yet also how similar.

Perhaps Julia hadn't married for the same reason Lucas

hadn't. Perhaps she could no more fall in love with a man than Lucas could fall in love with a woman.

"Tish . . . why did Julia never marry?"

"Because her suitors were all fortune hunters, like mine." Tish smiled wryly, sadly. "We fended them off together. It was . . . it wasn't a game, but Julia made it seem almost so." And then she said, "Why?"

"No reason," Tom said. The frustration returned. Or perhaps it was anger. *Lucas can't love a woman, and he won't love a man.* He kicked another stone.

Chapter Thirty-Two

THE ABBEY'S WALLED gardens were magnificent, even though it was winter and the flowers weren't blooming. Lucas liked the orderliness of everything—the vegetable beds laid out in rows, the carefully espaliered fruit trees, the sheltering walls. It felt peaceful and safe and serene. Afterwards, they had refreshments at the abbey, and it was clear that Cosgrove's chef was French. Lucas limited himself to three delicate chocolate-covered pastries, although he could have eaten ten.

He chewed slowly, and watched Tish and her new cousins. They were very easy with one another, clearly well on the way to becoming close friends.

Lucas contemplated a fourth pastry—and resolutely returned his attention to the three women: Lady Ware, blonde and pretty and vivacious; Lady Cosgrove, dark-haired and quietly friendly, almost as pregnant as Lady Ware; and Tish, angular and elegant. Try as he might, he could discern no family likeness between them.

"Next time you're in Devonshire, Kemp, we must spar," Cosgrove said, when they stood to leave.

"But only if you promise not to knock him out," Lady Cosgrove said hastily.

You needn't worry, Lucas almost told her. *He's only being polite.*

They strolled the half-mile back to Woodhuish House. The afternoon shadows were lengthening and the valley was as peaceful and serene as the walled gardens had been. Lucas found himself with Tish on his arm. He was glad. There was a question that had been nagging him all day. "Tish . . . did you give that chambermaid money?"

Tish glanced at him. "A little bit, yes. Would you rather I hadn't?"

Lucas struggled with his answer. If he said *No,* Tish would hear the lie. If he said *Yes,* he'd sound like a brute who wanted penniless women thrown out into the night to starve. "Seems like she was rewarded, rather than punished."

"I gave her enough for a fare to Exeter, so she can look for a new position. She's a foolish girl, and she brought her disaster upon herself, but you wouldn't want it to ruin her life, would you? You wouldn't want her to end up selling herself just so she can eat."

"No," he admitted, and it was the truth.

"I've got a stone in my shoe," Tish said, and halted.

Lucas halted, too, and waited while Tish took her shoe off, shook it upside down, put it back on, and retied the laces. By the time she was ready, the others were a hundred yards ahead, but Tish didn't hurry to catch up. She strolled slowly, her arm tucked through his. "Lucas? Do you remember what I said to you at Whiteoaks? About being careful?"

"Yes," Lucas said cautiously.

"I was wrong. *Don't* be too careful."

Lucas wrinkled his brow and looked at her. What was Tish talking about?

"Some people are meant to be together," Tish said. "Have you ever noticed that? You look at them together and you just *know* it."

Did she mean herself and Major Reid? "Yes," Lucas said.

"You and Tom are like that."

Lucas almost choked on his breath. What? He gave a laugh that was a little too hearty. "Well, we are best friends," he said, and changed the subject hurriedly. "How long are you and Reid staying here? You should come down to Pendarve afterwards. It's beautiful. The sea's almost on the doorstep."

Tish halted again. "Lucas."

Lucas halted, too, reluctantly. "Tish—"

"You and Tom are *meant* for each other, Lucas. You are *meant* to be together."

He stared at her, at her stern, serious face—and there was a long moment when his heart didn't beat, and his lungs didn't breathe, and no blood flowed in his veins. Everything stopped. He stood utterly still, unmoving, unbreathing. Tish was talking about more than friendship.

Tish *knew*.

He felt as if the ground had opened beneath his feet. He stood frozen in front of Tish, and yet he was also falling. And while he fell, the world disintegrated around him.

His heart started beating again—he heard it loudly in his ears—and blood was rushing fast and panicked in his veins— and Tish was still staring at him, her face more serious than he'd ever seen it.

Lucas swallowed, and moistened numb lips. "How do you know?"

"I saw you at the folly."

His world began to disintegrate even faster, collapsing around him. "Have you told anyone?"

"Of course I haven't!" Tish hesitated, and bit her lip, and then said, "Icarus was with me. He knows."

"Reid?" The word came out as a cry of anguish. Lucas swung away from Woodhuish House, from Reid walking a hundred yards ahead, and pressed his hands to his face. He wanted to die of shame, right there in the lane.

"It didn't seem to bother him," Tish said. "He was surprised, of course, but he took it quite calmly. He says that what you and Tom do is no one's business but your own."

Lucas lowered his hands and turned his head to look at her.

"Icarus is right. It isn't anyone's business but yours and Tom's. It's certainly none of *my* business. If he knew I was talking to you about it he'd be cross. But I had to tell you that what I said at Whiteoaks was wrong."

Lucas stared at her.

"You and Tom balance each other better than any two people I've ever seen."

Lucas swallowed. "Julia—"

Tish shook her head. "Tom balances you better than she ever did. Julia was your opposite; the two of you were like night and day. You and Tom aren't opposites. You're like . . . like morning and afternoon—and that's a stupid analogy, but what I'm trying to say is that you *complement* each other."

Lucas closed his mouth.

"Whenever you and Julia were in a room together, she took up nine-tenths of the space—and I don't mean she dominated you, because she *didn't*—she just took up your space without meaning to. I don't think either of you noticed it happened."

Lucas frowned at her, unsettled.

"Tom doesn't do that. He gives you room to be you."

Lucas glanced along the lane, at Tom.

"You talk more when you're with him, you laugh more, you're more *you*."

He brought his gaze back to Tish.

"You and Tom are meant to be together," Tish said, very seriously, like a magistrate passing judgment. "So, be careful, Lucas, but not *too* careful." And then she smiled and held out her hand to him.

Lucas took it.

They walked in silence for half a minute, and then Tish said, "I love you, Lucas."

"I love you, too," Lucas said.

They held hands all the way back to Woodhuish House. Tish told him about the puppy she and Reid had acquired and the man Reid was going into business with, an ex-sergeant with only one arm, but Lucas paid little attention. All he could think was: *Major Reid knows*. It made him feel ill—literally ill—as if he was going to cast up the contents of his stomach.

Tish knew about him and Tom—and for some reason it didn't matter that she knew—but it mattered that Reid knew. It mattered a lot. God, how was he going to look the man in the eye?

The feeling of nausea grew. It filled his belly and climbed his throat.

Tish stopped when they were close enough to see the patterns on the tall Tudor chimneys. "What is it, Lucas?"

I can't face Reid.

"Lucas?"

He shook his head, unable to tell her.

"Is it because Icarus knows?"

He thinks I'm a sodomite.

Tish didn't repeat the question; she waited silently, holding his hand.

Pressure built inside Lucas. Finally, he burst out: "He thinks we're back door ushers. And we're not! We don't do that! We're *not*."

Tish didn't ask what a back door usher was. Perhaps she knew what the term meant, perhaps she guessed. She looked at him gravely. "If you want me to tell him that, I will—but it won't change his opinion of you. He likes you."

"Likes me?" He pulled his hand free. "Christ, Tish! He thinks I'm a damned fool! They all do!"

Tish blinked. "Why on earth would anyone think that?"

"Because of last night. Because I made such a fuss, carrying on as if Tom was dying when it was just a bloody nose and a couple of bruises." They were being polite, pretending it hadn't happened—Sir Barnaby saying they were practically family, Cosgrove inviting him to spar—but behind the politeness they all knew he'd behaved like a hysterical old woman.

Tish pursed her lips. She glanced past him, at Woodhuish House, and then back at his face—and appeared to come to a decision. "You did exactly the right thing last night, Lucas. It *was* serious. His nose was broken, and both cheekbones, and one of his eye sockets."

"What?" Lucas said.

"And about a dozen bones in his hand."

"What?"

"You know how I have a knack for hearing lies? Well, Merry—Lady Ware, that is—also has a knack. Only hers is for nursing."

"What?" he said a third time.

"Lady Cosgrove has a knack, too. Charlotte. It runs in our family."

Lucas didn't say *What?* again, he just stared at her.

"No one thinks you're a fool. In fact, they seem to think

you're some kind of demigod. Barnaby calls you the Giant Slayer."

Giant Slayer? Me?

"I'll tell Icarus if you want me to, but it won't change his opinion of you. He *likes* you, Lucas."

Lucas looked away, down the valley.

"Do you want me to tell him?"

Lucas hesitated. Did he? Major Reid knew that he and Tom were lovers. How important was it that Reid knew they weren't sodomites?

"Lucas?"

He looked back at Tish, and shook his head.

Tish smiled. She held out her hand. "Shall we go inside?"

Lucas took her hand again. The urge to vomit wasn't as strong as it had been. He found himself able to climb the steps to the terrace.

Tish lowered her voice to a whisper. "I didn't tell you about Merry and Charlotte, all right? It's a family secret."

Chapter Thirty-Three

LUCAS WENT TO sleep not knowing what to do—and woke having decided. The post-chaise left Woodhuish House at nine o'clock. He spent the first forty miles examining his decision, laying it out in his mind like a clockmaker laying out the components of a clock—all the tiny cogs and springs and screws and shafts—all the possible consequences, the hazards and the risks. Then he reassembled his decision, putting the pieces back together until it formed a whole again.

It was a good decision. But not without its dangers.

He waited for the panic to come. It didn't. Instead, there was a feeling of calmness. Not a fatalistic calmness, but a deep and profound calmness that was almost serenity, and he knew —*knew*—that he'd made the right decision.

Lucas turned his attention to the question of when and where and how to tell Tom. Now? Once they reached Pendarve? Tonight over brandy? And should he mention the bank draft or not?

After ten miles, he was no closer to knowing, so he abandoned that line of thought.

He spent the next few miles thinking about Smollet—who quite likely knew, but didn't appear to mind—and about Robert—who possibly suspected, but also seemed not to mind—and about Tish and Reid—who definitely knew, and yet didn't mind at all.

And then he thought about Julia. Julia, who'd known him inside and out, who must have been aware of his feelings for Tom and had never said a word, who'd kept his secret for him.

He didn't need to wonder whether Julia would have approved of his decision; he knew it.

He looked across at Tom, sitting and staring out the window. The bruises under his eyes, on the bridge of his nose, were hardly discernible. By tomorrow they'd be gone. *Should I tell him now?* And then he looked past Tom and realized with a sense of shock that they had passed through Looe and were almost at Pendarve.

"Only a couple more miles," Lucas said. "You'll see it soon. It's built of stone and it's right on the water."

He sat anxiously, watching Tom's face. He wanted Tom to like Pendarve as much as he did.

The post-chaise slowed. To the left was a low stone wall, and beyond the wall was a tumble of rocks, and beyond that was the sea, gentle this afternoon, not pounding and sending up spray; to the right, the ground sloped up in a sheltering hill.

The post-chaise slowed still further, and rattled to a halt in front of Pendarve.

They climbed out. The salt tang of the ocean filled Lucas's mouth and nose, invigorating and fresh. God, he'd missed this smell. He inhaled deeply and watched Tom stretch his legs and examine their surroundings. Did he like the sea-smell? The gentle *slap-slap-slap* of the waves? What did he think of the house?

He tried to see the manor through Tom's eyes: the red and gray stone, the slate roof. Pendarve didn't have Whiteoaks' size, or its symmetry and crisp lines. He thought it looked rugged and comfortable, peaceful in its solitude—but perhaps Tom thought it looked bleak and isolated and small?

"What do you think?" Had Tom been expecting a mansion? "It's about a hundred times smaller than Whiteoaks."

"And I like it a hundred times more than Whiteoaks." Tom turned on his heel and looked out at the glinting silver-blue sea, the curve of coast with its pale shingle beaches and rocky reefs and windswept trees. "Look at that view."

"You like it?" Lucas said eagerly.

Tom gave him a look that said *Of course, I like it. I'd have to be insane not to.*

"Come inside," Lucas said. He turned and found Smollet standing at his elbow, and behind Smollet, the Teagues. "Oh, hello, Smollet. Good to see you."

"Good afternoon, Master Lucas, Master Tom." Smollet was as close to beaming as Lucas had ever seen him, his eyes crinkling, his mouth tucked up at the corners.

"Uh, this is Mrs. Teague, my housekeeper-cook," Lucas told Tom. "And Mr. Teague, who has charge of the stables and grounds. Smollet, can you pay off the postilions, please?"

"Of course, sir."

"Come inside," Lucas said again, taking Tom's arm.

"Sir?"

"Yes, Smollet?"

"I know you asked me to make the Green Room ready for Master Tom, but I took the liberty of preparing the Rose Room instead. It gets more sun."

Lucas glanced sharply at his manservant.

Smollet returned his gaze with utmost blandness.

"Er . . . thank you," Lucas said, and revised his assessment of Smollet, putting the man in the same category as Tish and Reid: He *definitely* knew—and he wasn't disturbed by it. Or maybe Smollet deserved a category of his own. If he'd prepared the Rose Room, with its adjoining door to Lucas's bedchamber, Smollet was actively encouraging them to spend their nights together.

Lucas ushered Tom inside, more than a little disconcerted.

By the time he'd shown Tom around the ground floor—tiny compared to Whiteoaks, but with a good library—his disconcertment had fallen away and he felt hopeful. Anxiously, eagerly, nervously hopeful. "Come upstairs."

He showed Tom the sewing room first. "My godfather's wife used this for embroidery." *Wouldn't it make a good studio? Look at all the light.* He held his breath, and watched as Tom crossed to the windows and looked out.

"Nice."

Lucas hugged that word to himself. He took Tom past the Green Room without opening the door, past his own bedchamber, and halted.

His nervousness grew even greater. "Um, this is your room."

He opened the door and let Tom step inside.

The room had belonged to his godfather's long-dead wife. It was decorated in rose-pink and cream.

"What do you think? There's a view straight out to sea. I usually sleep with my windows open a bit—even in winter. You can hear each wave. Um, my bedroom's through that door. This was my godfather's wife's room—Mrs. Warboys, her name was—that's why the door's there." He forced himself to stop gabbling, to take a breath. "Do you like it?" *It's yours, if you want it. Forever.*

Tom nodded.

"I'll have it redecorated. Your choice of color."

Tom looked at him, and lifted his eyebrows slightly. "My choice?"

Lucas nodded—and knew the moment had come. *Now* was the time to tell Tom and *here* was the place. And just as he'd known when and where, he knew how to tell him, too.

He'd *show* Tom. Show him in such a way that Tom could have no doubt he meant it.

Lucas stepped closer to Tom. His chest was tight. *Deeds speak more strongly than words,* he told himself.

Tom watched him. A little wary. Not saying anything.

"I want you to choose the color," Lucas said, and his voice was low and nervous and not quite steady. He took a deep breath, and reached out and took Tom by his waistband and pulled him closer. "Because I want this to be *your* room." *Your room, next to mine. Forever.*

He held Tom's gaze while he fumbled with the buttons of Tom's breeches, the buttons of his drawers. He held Tom's gaze while he wrapped his fingers around Tom's cock and stroked him. He held Tom's gaze while he knelt—and then he stopped concentrating on Tom's eyes and just concentrated on what it felt like to have the Corinthian in his mouth.

Intimate. It felt intimate. Each breath he took smelled of Tom. Tom's saltiness filled his mouth—his tongue rang with it, each taste bud reverberating. It felt profound. Not dirty or shameful, but wondrous. How could Tom's colonel have called this smoking a cheroot? This wasn't smoking a cheroot or playing a pipe or any of those stupid names people called it. This was telling a man that you loved him. *With my body I thee worship.*

After a moment, Tom's hands came to rest on his hair. Not gripping tightly, just a light touch, a second connection between them: Tom's cock in his mouth, Tom's hands gently cradling his skull.

Lucas caressed that helmet-like head with his tongue, learning its shape, its taste, its sleekness, and when he'd learned those things he started sucking in earnest, urging Tom towards ecstasy the way Tom had urged him so many times—and he knew *exactly* what it felt like to Tom—the wet heat of a mouth, the soft velvet tongue, the suction, the rhythm, the building pressure, the feeling that soon he'd *burst* with pleasure—and when Tom climaxed, Lucas swallowed his mettle without hesitation—tangy and hot—because it was Tom's and he loved Tom. All of him. Every part of him.

And then he stood and refastened Tom's clothing—tucking him into his drawers, buttoning his breeches—and put his arms around him and hugged him tightly. "I love you."

Tom stood quite still for several long seconds—and then he let out a sigh, and a deep core of tension seemed to dissolve in him. He bowed his head. "I never thought I'd hear you say that," he whispered into Lucas's shoulder.

"I'll say it every day from now on, if you wish."

Tom gave a shaky half-laugh. "Every second day will suffice."

Lucas tightened his embrace. "I've been in love with you since I was fourteen."

Tom was silent for a moment, and then he said, "It was sixteen, for me."

They stood leaning into each other for several minutes, not talking, just enjoying the closeness, and then Lucas pulled back, and looked at Tom. "This is your bedroom. Forever. You choose the color."

Tom gave a lopsided smile. There were tears in his eyes. "Blue," he said.

Afterwards

April 10ᵗʰ, 1810
Lincombe Park, Devonshire

AFTERNOON SUNLIGHT SHONE into the nursery, laying golden rectangles on the floor. A nursemaid sat in a rocking chair, quietly knitting, and alongside her were two cots. Lucas followed Tish across the room. He found himself tiptoeing.

Click click click, went the nursemaid's needles.

Lucas held his breath and stared down at the babies. Tish's twins. Tiny and pink and fast asleep. *Julia and I looked like this once.* He felt a pang of sadness, and waited for the feeling of having lost a limb, but it didn't come. Instead, he caught a fleeting scent of bergamot, as if Julia stood alongside him.

"Icarus says it's his fault. His grandfather was a twin, and his father."

Lucas nodded, and peered more closely at the babies. Which was the girl? Which the boy?

Tish turned to the nursemaid, middle-aged and comfortably plump. "Agnes, could you give us a few minutes' privacy, please?"

"Of course, ma'am."

The girl was the one on the right, Lucas decided, because her nose was a fraction tinier than her brother's.

"Lucas?"

He turned his head and looked at Tish. Motherhood suited her. She'd lost some of her angularity, acquired some curves, and she had a warm, soft, happy glow.

"Icarus and I have been discussing names. We'd like to call them Lucia and Julius. But only if you're happy with it."

Lucas took a breath—and found himself unable to speak.

He looked back at the sleeping twins. Tears filled his eyes. He blinked them away.

Lucia and Julius.

The faint scent of bergamot came again and he *knew* that Julia liked the names.

"And we'd like you and Tom to be their godfathers."

Godfathers. It was such a simple word, and yet it had such weight. Almost as much weight as *father.*

"Would you like that?"

Lucas nodded, and fumbled in his pocket for his handkerchief. "Yes," he managed to say.

"The christening is next month. Merry and Charlotte will be the godmothers."

Lucas nodded, and mopped his eyes and blew his nose. He gazed down at the babies. *Tom's and my godchildren.* "Will they have the same knack as you? With the lies?"

"Lucia will have one, but we won't know what it is until she's an adult."

Lucas stared at the two tiny faces. It was impossible to imagine them as adults. He had a strange, dizzying sense of possibilities opening out in all directions, and it took his breath away, rendered him speechless with wonder. All he could do was gaze down at them, Julius and Lucia, barely a month old, with their whole lives ahead of them.

THAT EVENING, WHILE he was tying his neckcloth, he heard a familiar *tap-tap* on the door. "Come in."

He watched in the mirror as Tom entered, dressed for dinner. Tom strolled over to the window. He didn't detour for a kiss, because Smollet was in the room. Smollet knew they were lovers—and they knew he knew—and Smollet knew they knew —but nothing had ever been said between them. It was a secret the three of them shared—a tacit collusion, an unspoken agreement. And part of keeping it secret was what they did now: behaving as nothing more than good friends in front of Smollet. The touches, the kisses, the endearments, were for when they were absolutely, utterly, unequivocally alone.

Tom sat on the broad windowsill and looked out at the gathering dusk and the distant glimmer of the ocean. He swung one foot idly. "I swear Tish's dog is even bigger than the last time we were here. If it wasn't as gentle as a milk-cow, I might have to be afraid of it."

Lucas finished with the neckcloth. Smollet helped him into his tailcoat.

"Done?" Tom asked.

"Done."

Smollet picked up Lucas's discarded clothes, laying them carefully over his arm. "Will there be anything else, Master Lucas?"

"No. Thank you, Smollet."

Tom stopped swinging his foot. He waited until Smollet had left the room, and then said, "Reid says they'd like to name the twins Julius and Lucia."

Lucas nodded.

"You all right with that?"

Lucas nodded again.

"He says they want us to be godfathers."

"Yes. Tish told me." And—damn it—he was teary-eyed for the second time that day.

Tom pushed away from the windowsill and hooked an arm around Lucas's neck and hugged him. Lucas hugged him back. He thought about Julia and felt the old sadness, and then he thought about Julius and Lucia. Who would they be? Not he and Julia, that was certain. They'd be their own unique selves. And he and Tom would watch over them. They'd hold the children's hands while they learned to walk, and pick them up when they fell, and carry them when they got tired. "It'll be almost like being parents."

"It will," Tom said. "And it'll be *fun*. We'll be the best godfathers ever!"

"We will." Lucas gave an unsteady laugh, and drew back from Tom's embrace. He wiped his eyes and checked his neckcloth in the mirror—slightly crooked—and then turned and looked Tom over.

He tweaked Tom's collar-points and straightened his neckcloth. Tom stood still and let him, a half-smile on his face.

Lucas smoothed Tom's lapels over his chest. There was a small, slim, hard rectangular shape over Tom's heart: a sketchbook. Lucas laid his hand on it, and thought of thin sheets of paper stopping musket balls. *Each day that I have with him is a gift.*

"I love you," he said quietly, even though he'd already told Tom that once today.

Tom's half-smile became a whole smile.

Lucas laughed with the sheer pleasure of being alive. He kissed Tom—quick and tender—and took Tom's wrist and tugged him towards the door. "Come on, we'll be late for dinner."

Author's Note

The Battle of Vimeiro, in Portugal, ended in French defeat—but rather than pursue their advantage, the British generals signed an armistice (the Convention of Cintra) that leaned heavily in France's favor. When news of this reached England, they were recalled for a court-martial.

The inquiry into the Convention of Cintra was held at the Royal College in Chelsea, London. General Wellesley, who had commanded the British troops to their victory at Vimeiro, arrived in England at the beginning of October. The inquiry began in November and was concluded in late December.

Wellesley, who signed the preliminary armistice under orders and had no part in negotiating the final convention, was completely cleared. He went on to command the British troops in Spain and Portugal—and ultimately to drive the French from the Iberian Peninsula.

Generals Dalrymple and Burrard, the authors of the convention, were also cleared, but never saw active service again.

Thank You

Thanks for reading *Claiming Mister Kemp*. I hope you enjoyed it!

If you'd like to be notified whenever I release a new book, please join my Readers' Group, which you can find at www.emilylarkin.com/newsletter.

I welcome all honest reviews. Reviews and word of mouth help other readers to find books, so please consider taking a few moments to leave a review on Goodreads or elsewhere.

Claiming Mister Kemp is the fourth book in the Baleful Godmother series. The earlier books are *Unmasking Miss Appleby*, *Resisting Miss Merryweather*, and *Trusting Miss Trentham*, and the subsequent ones are *Ruining Miss Wrotham* and *Discovering Miss Dalrymple*, with more to follow. I hope you enjoy them all!

Those of you who like to start a series at its absolute beginning may wish to read the series prequel—*The Fey Quartet*—a quartet of novellas that tell the tales of a widow, her three daughters, and one baleful Faerie.

The Fey Quartet and *Unmasking Miss Appleby* are available for free when you join my Readers' Group. Here's the link: www.emilylarkin.com/starter-library.

If you'd like to read the first two chapters of *Ruining Miss Wrotham,* the novel that comes next in the Baleful Godmother series, please turn the page.

Ruining Miss Wrotham

Chapter One

July 15th, 1812
London

Nell Wrotham had two godmothers. One had given her a
bible when she was christened and a copy of Fordyce's *Sermons
for Young Women* when she turned twelve. Her father had
insisted that Nell read the sermons and she had dutifully
obeyed.

Nell's second godmother hadn't given her a gift yet and
Nell's father hadn't known about her, because *that* godmother
was a Faerie and her existence was a deep, dark secret. Her
name was Baletongue and she would only come once, on
Nell's twenty-third birthday, and when she came she would
grant Nell one wish.

Nell was wishing as the stagecoach she sat in rattled

towards London. She was wishing that her twenty-third birthday had been yesterday, or perhaps today, or at the very latest, tomorrow. But it wasn't. She still had a week to wait.

She sat on the lumpy seat, pressed close by a stout widow on one side and an even stouter attorney's clerk on the other. Nell's fingers were neatly folded over her reticule, her expression calm, her agitation hidden. *A well-bred lady never shows her emotions*—one of the many maxims drilled into her by her father. Her father, whose rigid, unforgiving righteousness was at the root of this disaster.

Nell clutched her reticule more tightly and wished for the thousandth time that her birthday was sooner—and prayed that when her Faerie godmother finally came it wouldn't be too late.

Chapter Two

Mordecai Black reached London as the clocks were striking noon. The streets were dusty and the traffic sluggish. The air trapped between the buildings had a fetid undertone. He drew the curricle to a halt outside the Golden Cross Inn, thrust the reins at his groom, and jumped down.

The inn's yard thronged with porters and passengers, all of them hot and sweaty and irritable, but Mordecai had no difficulty traversing the crowd. People looked at him and prudently stepped aside.

The taproom was busy, the coffee room slightly less so. "Your master?" he asked a serving-man.

Mordecai followed the man's directions and found the innkeeper in a stuffy back office, bent over a ledger, tallying rows of numbers.

"The stagecoach from Bath that arrived this morning . . . are any of the passengers putting up here?"

The innkeeper looked up with a scowl on his brow, clearly annoyed by the interruption. He opened his mouth, took in Mordecai's size—and thought better of what he'd been about to say.

"A woman arrived this morning from Bath," Mordecai said. "Traveling alone. Is she staying here?"

"There was a woman." The innkeeper put aside his quill and reached for a smaller ledger. Not accounts, but room allocations. He ran his finger down the entries and halted at one.

Mordecai's heart began to beat faster, a drumbeat of hope and nervousness. He was acutely aware of the document tucked into his breast pocket.

"Mrs. Webster," the innkeeper said. "Yes, she's putting up here."

"Mrs. Webster?"

"Yes."

"It's Miss Wrotham I'm looking for."

The innkeeper closed the ledger. "Then she is staying elsewhere."

W, Mordecai thought. *Wrotham. Webster.* "What does she look like? Young, slim, dark brown hair?"

"I wouldn't call her young," the innkeeper said. "Or slim."

Mordecai's hopeful nervousness evaporated. In its place was a feeling that was part unease, part worry. He went outside to speak with the porters. Half a crown each and a glance at his face bought him their full attention.

Some days it annoyed him that his appearance intimidated people; today it was useful, but only one porter had noticed

Miss Wrotham. None of them had seen her leave the inn's yard.

Mordecai drove to Grosvenor Square, avoiding the other carriages by habit, scarcely noticing the landmarks. How the devil was he to find Miss Wrotham in a city the size of London?

The curricle rattled into the great square and there, on the far side, was his townhouse, a towering edifice with columns and a Palladian pediment and four rows of windows rising one above the other. Lord Dereham's house until eight months ago, and now Dereham's bastard's house. He'd heard the linkboys call it that—Dereham's bastard's house—not as a slur on his character, but merely acknowledging the truth of his birth: Dereham's natural son. Dereham's bastard.

Mordecai drew the curricle to a halt and clambered stiffly down. The hours he'd spent on the road were catching up with him: the journey to Bath, the journey back again, no rest in between.

"Take it round to the stables," he told the groom. "Have the rest of the day off."

The curricle clattered away over the cobblestones, but Mordecai didn't climb the steps to his front door.

Miss Wrotham was somewhere in London. Alone.

Mordecai stripped off his gloves and rubbed his face, felt grit and sweat and stubble. He needed food, a shave, a cold bath, fresh clothes. And maybe a nap.

He turned on his heel and stared across the square, seeing tall buildings, hazy rooftops, chimneys. The city seemed suddenly full of dangers. He felt a twinge of fear—an emotion he was unused to. He stood six foot five and weighed two hundred pounds and he knew how to fight, he was *good* at fighting, but Miss Wrotham was none of those things. And she was female, and alone in London without friends or protectors, and she had no experience of abbesses and cutpurses and bullyboys.

The sense of fear became stronger, laced with anxiety. *Where the blazes is she?*

Behind him, he heard his front door open. Mordecai looked around. His butler peered down the steps at him. "Sir?"

"I'm going for a walk."

HE WENT TO Halfmoon Street, five minutes' fast walk from Grosvenor Square. The Dalrymples' house was closed and shuttered, the knocker removed from the door—they were away, but Miss Wrotham *must* have known that; the Dalrymples were her cousins and she knew as well as anyone that they spent every summer in the country. So why had she come to London, and how the devil was he to find her?

Mordecai hesitated on the doorstep of the shuttered house, sweating, tired, worried. God, it was warm in London, the air close and still and sticky, no breeze to ease the heat.

He loosened his neckcloth and rubbed his face again, stubble rasping under his hand. There was one other person Miss Wrotham knew in London.

Mordecai strode around to Berkeley Square telling himself that he was a fool, that the last person Miss Wrotham would visit was Roger—the man had jilted her, for God's sake!

Halfmoon Street to Berkeley Square took all of two minutes. Mordecai's pace slowed when he neared Roger's house. It was a handsome building, but not as handsome as his own townhouse, nor as large.

He wondered what the linkboys called it.

Mordecai halted at the foot of the steps. *A fool's errand, this. Roger won't know, and if he did, he'd delight in not telling me.* And then he felt the prickling anxiety again. He touched his fingertips to the marriage license in his breast pocket, took a deep breath, and climbed the steps of the new Lord Dereham's house.

The butler opened the door.

"Afternoon, Bolger. My cousin in?"

The butler's lips tightened at the word *cousin*, a tiny spasm of distaste. He looked as if he wished he had permission to close the door in Mordecai's face. "Lord Dereham is at home, sir," he said woodenly.

"I'll see him."

The entrance hall was similar to Mordecai's own: the high ceiling molded and painted by Robert Adam, the long stretch of marble floor, the doors to dining room, drawing room, and library on either side, the staircase at the end. There the resemblance ended; Mordecai didn't decorate his entrance hall with footmen. Vases were decoration, a Robert Adam ceiling was decoration, but his footmen were not. Roger's footmen were, poor sods. Four of them stood in their curling wigs and gold-braided livery, two on either side of the hall, backs to the wall, chins up, eyes staring blankly ahead. Human statues. Mordecai almost snorted. *Why in God's name must he have one standing here all day, let alone four?*

But he knew the answer: the footmen were because Roger liked to flaunt his wealth, and there were four because Roger liked symmetry. Two footmen would have been too few, and three or five unacceptable.

"Lord Dereham is momentarily occupied," the butler said,

his expression dyspeptic, as if Mordecai's kinship to his master pained him as much as it pained Roger. "If you will step into the library, I shall inform him of your arrival." He gave a stiff-necked nod, and one of the footmen sprang to open the library door.

Mordecai had taken half a dozen steps towards the library, wondering how long the butler and Roger would choose to keep him waiting, when the drawing room door opened abruptly and a young lady strode out. "—hiding behind excuses. A *hen* has more courage than you!"

Mordecai halted.

He'd been truly and deeply surprised twice in his life. Once, when his father had come to claim him, and the second time when Henry Wright had stood up for him at Eton. This moment qualified as the third. He was so astonished that he gaped. Eleanor Wrotham was here? In Roger's house?

"If you won't help me, I'll find someone who has the gumption to do so!" Miss Wrotham was magnificent in her scorn, eyes flashing, voice ringing, cheeks flushed.

And then he saw the tears trembling on her eyelashes. She wasn't merely angry; she was upset.

Miss Wrotham didn't see him. She crossed the entrance hall briskly, flung open the door before Bolger could reach it, and marched outside.

Roger emerged from the drawing room—red-faced and righteous, his blond hair sleek with pomade. Mordecai ignored his cousin. He strode after Miss Wrotham and shut the door firmly in Bolger's face. "Miss Wrotham!" He took the steps two at a time.

Miss Wrotham halted on the flagway and glanced back. He saw surprise cross her face—a brief, wide-eyed flare of astonishment—and then the surprise snuffed out and she was once again her father's daughter, haughty and aloof.

Mordecai stared down at her and knew in his bones that she was the one woman in all the world whom he was meant to marry. Not because of her appearance and her breeding—those had been Roger's reason for offering for her—but because of what lay beneath those things: the clear-eyed intelligence, the suppressed passion, the spirit bursting to be free.

He trod down the last three steps. "I'll help you," he said. "Whatever it is, I'll help."

Miss Wrotham's eyebrows lifted slightly. She looked him up and down.

Mordecai was suddenly acutely aware of what he must look like: sweaty, hulking, unshaven, dressed in clothes that had been elegant yesterday, but today were wrinkled and travel-stained.

He resisted the urge to tighten his neckcloth and brush the dust from his coat, but it was impossible not to feel embarrassed. Of all the ways he'd imagined meeting Miss Wrotham again, this wasn't one of them. He felt a faint blush creep into his cheeks—and when was the last time he'd blushed? Years ago.

Mordecai endured her scrutiny, and wished he knew what Miss Wrotham thought of him. Not what she thought of his appearance—it was obvious what anyone would think of his appearance right now—but what she thought of *him*. Mordecai Black. Earl's son. Bastard.

Society accepted him—his father's sponsorship had seen to that—but not everyone liked him. Roger certainly didn't. Miss Wrotham's father—a high stickler—hadn't either. He'd thought Mordecai unworthy of his daughter's hand, but the man was dead now and the only opinion that mattered was Miss Wrotham's. What did *she* think? Did those astute eyes see past his reputation as a rake? Did she see who he truly was?

Perhaps she did, because instead of turning away from

him as a prudent and respectable young woman should, Miss Wrotham said, "I need to go to Seven Dials, but none of the jarveys will take me—they say it's no place for a lady."

Seven Dials? Mordecai stared at her in astonishment. "They're correct."

"Will you take me there, Mr. Black?"

"No." He shook his head emphatically. "Absolutely not. If you have business there, allow me to go in your stead."

"I have to go myself."

"Seven Dials is little more than taverns and brothels," Mordecai told her bluntly. "It's not a place you should visit."

"My sister's there." Miss Wrotham's aloofness slipped. Desperation and urgency were clear to read on her face. "She's in terrible trouble. She needs my help."

Mordecai's eyebrows lifted. The sister who'd plunged the Wrotham family into disgrace? Who'd ruined Miss Wrotham's marriage prospects and caused Roger to jilt her? "Is this the sister who, er . . ." *Ran off with a soldier.*

"I have only one sister."

And whatever that sister had done, Miss Wrotham obviously still cared about her.

Mordecai hesitated. If Miss Wrotham's sister was in Seven Dials, then her fortunes had sunk very low. "I'll bring her to you. It's best that you don't—"

"I'm going with you."

"Miss Wrotham—"

"Mr. Black, you would terrify her!"

Mordecai felt himself flush. "I assure you that I'll treat your sister with respect," he said stiffly.

"It's not that," Miss Wrotham said, with an impatient wave of her hand. "Oh, don't you see? You look *dangerous,* and she's scared enough as it is . . . and I *have* to go with you. She's my sister!"

Mordecai looked down at her and saw fierce determination on her face and stubbornness in the set of her chin—the spirit he'd admired last year, no longer suppressed but burning brightly. And then he thought of trying to persuade a frightened young woman who didn't know him from Adam to trust him enough to get in a carriage with him. He grimaced inwardly.

"Please," Miss Wrotham said, and she reached out and touched his arm, a gesture that was somehow both reckless and cautious at the same time, as if she thought that merely laying her hand on his sleeve might ruin her.

Mordecai's awareness of her flared. The last of his resolve crumbled. He gave a reluctant nod. "We'll go together."

Relief and hope illuminated Miss Wrotham's face—and then the urgency returned. She gripped his arm, her fingers digging deeply into his sleeve. "Can we go now? Where's your carriage?"

"In the stables. A hackney will be quicker."

"They'll refuse—"

"They'll not refuse me."

Like to read the rest?
Ruining Miss Wrotham is available now.

Acknowledgments

A number of people helped to make this book what it is. Foremost among them is my sterling developmental editor, Laura Cifelli Stibich, but I also owe many thanks to my hardworking copyeditor, Maria Fairchild, and eagle-eyed proofreader, Martin O'Hearn.

The cover and the series logo are both the work of the talented Kim Killion, of The Killion Group. Thank you, Kim!

And last—but definitely not least—my thanks go to my parents, without whose support this book would not have been published.

Emily Larkin grew up in a house full of books—her mother was a librarian and her father a novelist—so perhaps it's not surprising that she became a writer.

Emily has studied a number of subjects, including geology and geophysics, canine behavior, and ancient Greek. Her varied career includes stints as a field assistant in Antarctica and a waitress on the Isle of Skye, as well as five vintages in New Zealand's wine industry.

She loves to travel and has lived in Sweden, backpacked in Europe and North America, and traveled overland in the Middle East, China, and North Africa.

Emily enjoys climbing hills, yoga workouts, watching reruns of Buffy the Vampire Slayer and Firefly, and reading.

She writes historical romances as Emily Larkin and fantasy novels as Emily Gee. Her websites are www.emilylarkin.com and www.emilygee.com.

Never miss a new Emily Larkin book. Join her Readers' Group at www.emilylarkin.com/newsletter and receive free digital copies of *The Fey Quartet* and *Unmasking Miss Appleby*.

OTHER WORKS

THE BALEFUL GODMOTHER SERIES

The Fey Quartet (Series Prequel)

Maythorn's Wish ~ Hazel's Promise

Ivy's Choice ~ Larkspur's Quest

Original Series

Unmasking Miss Appleby

Resisting Miss Merryweather

Trusting Miss Trentham

Claiming Mister Kemp

Ruining Miss Wrotham

Discovering Miss Dalrymple

Garland Series

(Coming soon)

OTHER HISTORICAL ROMANCES

The Earl's Dilemma

My Lady Thief

Lady Isabella's Ogre

The Midnight Quill Trio

The Countess's Groom

The Spinster's Secret

The Baronet's Bride

FANTASY NOVELS

(Written as Emily Gee)

Thief With No Shadow

The Laurentine Spy

The Cursed Kingdoms Trilogy

The Sentinel Mage ~ The Fire Prince ~ The Blood Curse